SUCKER FOR PAYNE

CARRIE THOMAS

To those who change their path.

PROLOGUE

CONNER

ONE MORE DRINK. It was always one more.

Jared's patio creaked under my weight, as I shuffled across the deck. My concentration focused in on how every other step skipped the bowed boards, leaving me a bit unsteady.

Jared pointed to the half-empty bottle in my grip and asked, "You up for a round of golf tomorrow?"

"Sure, I'll take your money." I shrugged as I took a swig of the whiskey.

Jared grinned. "Five hundred?"

A gorgeous blonde, who stood close enough to hear us, licked her lips, and her dark eyes widened as she edged closer to Jared's back. The first stirrings of anger rose in my chest as her red nails tapped a rhythm against her bottle of Stella. I didn't have to look up to know all party-goers were watching us. I could feel their curious gazes on me.

I leaned in close enough, so only he would hear. "I hate it when you do shit for show." Straightening, I took another pull and slammed the bottle on the table. "A thousand." I turned my back to his audience and stumbled down the wooden stairs.

I had rounded the corner of his house before he finally accepted. I knew he would. His ego wouldn't allow him to be one-upped in front of his friends.

The mid-November chill bit at my fingertips as the engine in my old pick up roared to life. It ran like a champ, but the heater had bitten the dust two years ago. My left leg bounced automatically, knowing the movement would help keep me warm for the short drive.

After clearing a red light, I leaned over to open my glove compartment. Hank Williams Jr. would do, since I didn't want to hear my own thoughts. And given that the radio had joined the heater only a couple of weeks ago, it wasn't like I had much choice, if I didn't want to sit in silence. The discs shifted to the right, almost out of reach. I kept my left hand on the stirring wheel and leaned further into the seat, so I could snag the CD with my free hand.

I straightened up to the sound of screeching tires. The bright lights of the car I was about to hit head-on blinded me. My thigh cramped from the amount of force my foot applied to the brake pedal. I jerked the wheel toward the ditch, but wasn't going fast enough. Loud honks from a small car echoed in the cab of my truck. The frightened eyes and shocked face of the other driver filled my vision as my body rose from the seat.

I floated in that millisecond, before time started again, causing my body to jerk and twist freely about the cab. The other driver's hands rose up, as if he could block the impact. Shards of glass exploded with a deafening roar, each razor-sharp piece digging into my skin as the truck began to flip. My head slammed into the side window as the truck rolled over, causing me to black out.

WILLOW

One more pill. It was always one more.

I opened my eyes, barely able to focus. Between the partying we'd done the night before, and the darkness, I couldn't even make out who was in bed with me. I rolled over, hoping to find Chase.

Long black hair.

Purple nails.

Naked breasts splayed out for anyone to see.

Nope. Not Chase.

Easing myself up, I squinted at the hangover bulldozing its way into my brain, and looked around the room. Bodies lay haphazardly on the floor and a worn-out sofa; some were clothed, some not so much. But all were blitzed.

I wasn't familiar with the home, being that last night was the first night Chase had invited me to his frequent hang-out. Our fights had escalated over the past month, and I believed he intended on making nice with me by allowing me to party with his friends. He constantly told me how I couldn't handle them, and it was best for him to keep his girlfriend and his friends separate. I disagreed.

Heaviness plagued my legs, and bile rose from my stomach with each room I passed. I coughed as the mixture of smoke and sweat passed through my nostrils. Goosebumps trailed down my legs when my right foot slipped in something slimy on the hardwood floors. I caught myself on the wall and shivered.

Feeling for the door frame ahead, I sighed when I finally reached carpet. I wiped my foot back and forth until the slime was gone. However, the relief was short lived, as I locked gazes with not only my boyfriend, but some girl named Maria; the one he'd told me was his cousin. I assumed that was a lie . . . given their present position and all.

"Come join us, babe," Chase slurred.

"I thought she was your cousin." I should have been yelling and screaming. I should have been throwing things at him, or cussing her out, but I didn't. I spoke calmly, and direct.

"Nah, we just tell people that. No one ever understands our relationship," blondie said as she continued to ride my boyfriend.

"Babe, don't—uh." He groaned and his hands squeezed her thighs as he pulled her back down over him.

I glanced at the nightstand, where a small mirror laid on top. It was covered with white powder cut into lines. To the right of the powder, three prescription bottles were knocked over on their sides, with pills spilled out haphazardly.

I narrowed my eyes at Chase, livid that he was in the middle of what appeared to be ecstasy, while my heart was being ripped out of my chest. He couldn't even finish his sentence, or stop fucking a girl I'd believed to be his family, to try to explain why he was cheating on me.

His face was contorted like a cartoon character; hers in a sinister smile. I hated them. I hated me.

Hastily, I reached the night stand and grabbed the first handful of pills I could reach. I shoved them in my mouth as fast as I could. I swallowed hard, forcing the pills down my dry throat. Neither of them noticing, I left the room and returned to the bed I'd woken up in. Folding my knees up to my chest, I waited for the effects from whatever I'd taken to kick in. I wasn't sure what I wanted to feel, but I was certain I wanted to stop the heaviness in my heart. My eyes fluttered twice as I pulled the ripped blanket up to separate me and the naked girl who laid beside me.

I awoke to a nurse poking my arm, shaking her head as she tried to find my stubborn vein. I took in her expression, her frustration plain as day. Once she realized I was conscious, she didn't even bother to ask how I was doing.

"Hey." My mom's strained voice broke through the silence.

Her red-rimmed eyes were glossy, and her voice was scratchy, almost as if she hadn't spoken in a while. I licked my parched, cracked lips, not knowing what to say. I was perfectly aware that I'd almost taken my own life. I remembered it all too well, wishing like hell I could forget it.

"Willow," she cried. "Please let me help you."

I remained silent, not wanting to have the heart-to-heart I so desperately needed, especially in front of a stranger. The older nurse finished drawing my blood, then stuck a Band-Aid on my arm. Upon her exit, I turned back to my mom. My poor mother, who'd done nothing but love me and raise me on her own, sometimes working two jobs to keep a roof over our heads, and food in our tummies.

Tears spilled from my eyes. Humiliation crippled me. Guilt ate away at my insides, knowing that no matter what I said, it'd never take away the pain I'd caused her. No amount of apologies would ever take back the recklessness I'd had with my own life, not thinking for one moment about hers. I wasn't sure when I'd become that person. The selfish one who, for not one second, ever considered anyone else's feelings.

"I'm sorry." I couldn't help but avert my eyes.

The hospital bed dipped as she sat down and wrapped her arms around me, pulling me in so tight, it was hard to inhale. Instinct told me to pull away, so I could take a deep breath, but my heart wouldn't allow it. My heart wanted my mom.

"How long?" I hadn't a clue how long I'd even been there.

"Five hours." She straightened her sweater, tugging at a loose button. While she struggled with her words, I kept thinking about how stupid I'd been. Had I not gotten to a hospital, I would have been dead.

"I need help." Those words were the heaviest I'd ever spoken, yet they almost made me feel weightless. I'd never let something so personal escape me before. I'd always carried my shame deep, knowing I'd take the decisions I'd made to the grave. Admitting my loss of control scared me, because once I said it out loud, it became real. The repercussions were tangible, and simply existing in the shadows of everyday life wouldn't be an option anymore. I couldn't take it back. I couldn't tell her I'd only been joking.

She hugged me again, and I knew, no matter what happened from that point forward, I didn't want to die before she did. The grief and sorrow surrounding her like a black cloud of smoke crushed me. I never wanted to be the cause for such pain in her eyes, ever again.

CHAPTER 1
CONNER
(TEN YEARS LATER...)

I SILENTLY COUNTED my reps on the bench. *Three. Two. One.* I continued to push through the pain, not caring in the slightest that I was probably shredding my shoulder.

Sitting up, I grabbed my towel from the floor and wiped my face. Just as I was about to turn up the volume on my iPod, Trevor Steele's shadow hovered over me, patiently waiting for me to acknowledge him. I nodded in greeting.

His chin lifted slightly. "What's up?"

"Same shit," I blew out a breath, "different day."

His mouth turned downward, but not quite forming a frown. He tucked his hands in the pockets of his black sweats and nodded toward the vacant octagon in the center of the gym. "Why don't you come to the cage tonight?"

I grunted. "Not ready."

Steele nodded.

I hated, yet fully accepted, the fact he understood. At first, I'd questioned his friendship. The first day I'd walked into the newly built gym, he'd struck up a conversation with me. It took a couple of weeks, but once I figured out he hadn't wanted anything from me, and that I could trust him, I gave in some.

The sky-high wall of armor I'd built up over the years still very much existed, but he'd chipped away at it a little each day, until one day, I actually laughed. He told me about a fight he'd had before he'd gone pro, where he'd wailed on his opponent until the poor guy's mother made her way down to the edge of the cage and begged him to stop. I couldn't imagine. The dude was a grown-ass man.

Steele owned the gym—had saved for nearly five years for it. I respected him and his work ethic. Over time, I'd learned he came from humble beginnings. His father had skipped town, leaving him and his mom to rely on government housing, as she worked two jobs to put food on the table. The only reason he even became interested in martial arts was because a preacher offered free lessons at the local community center. His determination was valiant, and his chill vibes were inviting. It wasn't hard to be around him, and that was appealing to me.

Not that I'd been looking for a friend, but he thought like I did. Our lives had been so different, yet we were similar at our core. He never asked for anything more than I was willing to share, but was able to draw the correct conclusions when I stayed silent.

"You have to get back out there, man." He hit his fist on the bar I'd been using. "Blow off some steam, and make a few bucks in the meantime."

"Yeah, maybe." I leaned over with my elbows on my thighs to hide my face. "It's not like I'm getting my hands on any of the money I had prior to the conviction. And I'm not getting any other offers with a felony on my record."

Steele grimaced. "Still no resolution?"

"Nah." After being released from prison, I'd contacted my old lawyer, hoping he'd be able to shed some light on my partnership with Jared—who hadn't contacted me once while I was locked up. Turned out, Jared had dissolved our contract.

Steele whistled through his teeth and shook his head.

I shrugged. "Papers said any money we had would be split fifty-fifty, but there's nothing to split after he spent all of it. I won't fight it though. I want nothing more to do with courtrooms or lawyers. I've made peace with what my life has become."

"You don't miss that life at all?"

I shook my head, thinking about my years spent flipping homes.

"Not really. I mean, I couldn't get a loan now anyways. But coming back to so little, after all the hard work I put in, sucked."

What little I did have after my release went to a civil lawsuit. I'd only countered twice, before the boy's mom involved in my accident accepted. I just wanted to be done with it all, naively thinking that settling would give me closure on the whole ordeal. I'd been wrong.

Steele sat down on the bench across from me. "So, you'll think about it?"

I gulped down some water before answering. "Don't know yet."

He smacked my shoulder. "Come on, man."

"Fact is, I do need an income. The little I had from selling the house is almost shot."

"See?" Steele brightened. "This is perfect."

"I don't know if I'm ready to commit to something, other than going to the gym and home. I need to regroup and adapt to my surroundings." I wiped away the sweat forming on my upper lip. "Get used to being free."

Free. Simple, yet profound. Symbolic, yet not true. I'd never be free. Not from the memory, and sure as fuck not from the guilt.

"I get it," Steele said.

I huffed a laugh laced with pain and guilt. "I've been off parole for nearly a month, and still don't know what to do with myself." I hated how my voice softened with the rising emotions.

Steele clasped his hands between his knees and leaned forward. "How long were you on parole?"

"Two years," I said. "I met with my PO every week, making sure my paperwork was up to date, then worked eight hours a day at the mission outreach."

In that time, even though I'd met other guys in the same situation I'd been in, I hadn't connected with any of them. They all wanted to discuss their situations, almost like therapy sessions. I had no intention of ever talking about it again. It was shitty enough re-playing the accident in my mind every time I closed my eyes. The last thing I wanted to do was relive it with a live audience.

"That should count for something," he said.

I raised an eyebrow at him. "I come to this gym because I've got nothing else to do. I tried fixing things in the house I rent. I've even cleaned the yard up, and planted a few twigs I dug up from ditches. But nothing calms my nerves like a workout."

"That's a good thing," Steele said with a grin. "I'm the same way."

I placed my sweatshirt in my bag. "I've made too many mistakes, man."

"We all have. You're human."

"No, not normal mistakes."

"You know we're cool, yeah? You're a good dude, Conner."

"I don't think you understand. I was partying one night and hit a kid head on," I said, deliberately trying to scare him away. "I killed him." He knew I'd been locked up, but he hadn't known the reason.

He crossed his arms and tilted his head down. I never looked away, willing him to meet my stare. Deep down, I hoped it wouldn't change his view of my character, but at the same time, I knew I didn't deserve the free pass.

He looked back at me, silent for a few moments. "That really sucks. I'm sorry you experienced that."

"It is what it is. I drove impaired nearly every day for years; even before I could legally drink." I shook my head. "But I can't fix what happened. I can't fix anything." I zipped my bag, completely over the confession. It didn't matter anyhow.

"No, you can't fix everything, you're right. But you *can* take what time you have left here and do something positive with it. People make mistakes, man. You made one."

I rolled my eyes, not meaning to be disrespectful, but I'd made a hell of a lot more than one.

He stood at the same time I did, knowing I was leaving. "It was a mistake that will affect you for the rest of your life, but there are ways to deal with tragedies, while still living a life worth living. Don't quit. Don't give up on your life like that. There is a reason you're still here. Don't waste it. I mean it. You have potential, Conner. Even if you don't want to do this forever, fighting is an outlet for you, and you're good at it. Do something with the opportunity."

I huffed a breath. "I'll think about it."

Steele nodded in victory and slapped my shoulder on his way toward the back of the room.

To say Steele's pep talk was successful would be an understatement. In fact, it only took me two days to weigh the pros and cons. Turned out, there weren't many cons. Four weeks later, I entered the cage for the first time. Overcome with an emotion I still couldn't pin down, I felt like I was soaring with every punch landed. My insides rolled, exhilaration oozed from my pores. It was as if my body had duplicated, one hovered above, floating, while the other, feet firmly planted on the ground, physically endured the fight. It was a complete out-of-body experience.

I'd sparred with Steele multiple times in the past, but nothing compared to going all out in a bout. I found release in it. My body relaxed, even though I was tense. My mind calmed, almost to the point where I wasn't thinking at all. I'd never experienced anything like it before. Once I found a flow, a passion developed for the sport—for something other than drowning my sorrows, or longing to feel numb. It was something I could put all my energy into. Something positive for a change.

I spat blood onto the mat, then licked my sticky lips. The initial shock energized me. Warmth flowed through my body, as tingles shot from the top of my head, down to my bare feet. I stood still, allowing the adrenaline to seep through my veins like a junkie in an alleyway. In the middle of letting someone knock my insides around, I was at my calmest. Tranquil, despite the intense concentration I had on my opponent.

I grinned at Kramer's dumbfounded expression, and the split skin stung. The pain—an agony that demanded to be felt. Every punch, every kick, every bruise, only added to the euphoria I had.

I'd initially been in the mood to go a few rounds with Kramer, but the longer I had to look at his face, the more he pissed me off. I lurched forward, giving him the full-fledged power of my Superman punch. I hadn't trained much for the fight, knowing I could make him tap within the first three minutes if I'd wanted to.

His feet were heavy; his stance upright. He was cocky for no reason. It made me think he was a nutcase. Not like me. No, crazier than me, because at the end of the day, I was good at fighting. He was getting into cages with fighters who could kill him. He was an idiot. Certifiable. And I had zero tolerance for him.

The fact that I had to fight him in the first place annoyed me. I'd wanted a challenge, one that would push my adrenaline over the edge and exhaust me. The unlucky son-of-a-bitch who was pulling money tonight would be pissed. They'd already talked to me last week about drawing it out for the crowd. Ticket sales would go down, if the crowd didn't feel they were getting their money's worth. Even though Steele allowed the fights to take place in his gym, he steered clear of the money being exchanged; that way, his hands were clean if word ever got out to the pro league.

I turned my back to the crowd, when the referee took my arm, raising it high in the air, signaling I'd won. As if anyone watching the fight needed someone to tell them who'd won. I'd knocked his ass out. Everyone witnessed it. Why did I have to stand there like a fucking movie star, when everyone cheered me on like my life would end if they didn't? I despised the empty appreciation. I hadn't cured cancer. I hadn't captured America's Most Wanted. I'd simply punched someone so hard, he'd fallen like a ton of bricks onto a mat.

"Hell yeah, man! I've never seen a Superman punch so fluid in my life. You nailed that son-of-a-bitch. Even if Lopez were here watching, he'd never be ready for you next week. No amount of scouting will prepare him for that." Steele slapped me on the shoulder, already looking ahead to my next fight.

I blew out a breath I hadn't realized I was holding. I needed to get out. I had the sudden urge of flight; my anxious energy surging on the inside, bubbling at my core, preparing to explode. "Thanks. I'm going to head out. You need anything?"

His brow furrowed at my nonchalance. It wasn't that I was trying to be a dick, quite the contrary. I'd deliberately kept my response short, not wanting to express the growth of my anxiety. My pulse thrummed double time as my heart rate sped up, and my mind raced with thoughts of consumption. I didn't want Steele to know I cared more about numbing myself than I did celebrating a win with him.

I pulled my sweatpants on over my shorts, thinking about how a whiskey would burn going down. No matter how hard I tried, I couldn't stop the soft whisper. Instant gratification was a mind-fuck. Because the second that instant was gone, shame and disappointment would flood the void. For me to have such will-power physically, I was a pussy mentally. Giving in to the impulse made me feel weak. My brain never rested. The desire was always there, pushing and pulling, keeping me off balance. There was never a day where I didn't feel compelled to do it—to give in to the urge.

CHAPTER 2
WILLOW

"WILLOW!" Andy shoved my office door open so hard it banged against the wall. "I need you to cover that cage fight at Steele's Gym on Fifth Avenue tonight."

"Why?"

"John's sick," he said in a rush as he continued toward the windows. His nervous energy buzzed between us and made my scalp prickle.

"You do realize I write about feminism, right?" I tapped a set of papers on the desk. "What the hell am I going to talk to a bunch of meatheads about?"

His head turned sharply from the city streets below toward me. "How about the fight?" He folded the papers he held in his hands.

"I know nothing about cage fighting," I said with a huff. "Hell, I'm not sure it's even legal."

"Look, just take some notes, make it a simple piece, I don't care. You're good at making something out of nothing." He rushed out of my office, dropping the papers on my desk as he passed, not caring in the least where they landed.

"Fine, but you owe me," I muttered. Picking up the loose papers, I saw that they were leave requests for two individuals in my office. I shook my head, and stacked them neatly to the side. I'd drop them off at HR when I left for the day.

I knew he was stressed because of the current deadline we were on, but I'd never seen him so out of sorts. I shook off the worries, and thought about what he'd just asked me to do. I took a deep breath, attempting to calm my nerves. Writing about something I knew nothing about worried me. My name would be on the piece. He would have to approve it, and of course, I wanted to do a good job.

I glanced at the clock. If I cut out early, I would have time to do some research. I shut my computer off and grabbed my bag, deciding a little research was better than none. I hadn't been advised about who was fighting, and I couldn't even google the names before showing up at the event. My annoyance with Andy only grew as I approached Interstate 214, enroute to my house to freshen up. Lena, my best friend, texted me on my way home wanting to go out for dinner. After I told her about my change of plans, she insisted on meeting me there, explaining that she didn't want to miss any action.

I still wasn't sure what to expect when I arrived early, and parked my car under the only street light I could find. The click of my heels against the pavement echoed off the graffiti-covered building as I crossed the street in front of Steele's Gym. I continued to take in my surroundings, as I quickened my steps to the front door.

"Ten bucks," the guy outside the door said.

"Doesn't the gym offer a professional courtesy to media?" I asked.

He snorted and shook his head as he stuck out a hand and wiggled his thick fingers.

I blew out a frustrated breath and dug through my wallet, trying to buy time to come up with a plan that didn't involve me going in search of an ATM.

Tears stung my eyes as soon as I felt a crumpled bill's edge behind my license. *Oh, Mom. Bless your heart. Always taking care of me.* She couldn't seem to help hiding cash in my wallet these days. I handed him the twenty and blinked hard as I waited for my change.

I shot Lena a text to warn her to bring cash, then entered through the massive, tinted-glass door. It was lighter inside than it looked from the outside. It didn't look like much more than a warehouse from the street, but the interior was sophisticated, fresh, and appeared to be high end.

Rows of bleachers surrounded a black octagon. On the north end of the cage, black netting separated what appeared to be expensive workout equipment. Someone had definitely put some money into the gym. I assumed the fights that took place were under the table; I'd have to follow up on that. But I'd never heard of them, and didn't believe men would pummel each other for fun, so it didn't seem that far-fetched.

My wandering gaze halted when I witnessed some money exchanging hands. Apparently, my observations didn't go unnoticed, because before I could take my pen out, a huge man in khaki slacks and a plain gray T-shirt approached me. I liked his style. His red Vans stuck out, making him seem younger than he probably was.

"Trevor Steele." He held his hand out for me to shake.

"Willow Stevens." I smiled, placing my hand in his. "Nice to meet you."

"Your first time here?"

"Am I that transparent?"

His chuckle surprised me. "Nah, I'm just always around. I would have remembered you."

"Well, I heard about the fights and wanted to see what all the buzz was about." Offering my Daily News media badge hadn't helped at the door, so I didn't see any point in pulling it out for him.

"Oh yeah?" Trevor said. "What are you into? Boxing? Grappling? Jiu-jitsu?"

Ju who? I crossed my arms, aiming to protect myself from his curious questions. "Grappling," I answered.

"Lucky for you, that's Payne's specialty."

"Cool. I'm looking forward to it." I smiled, trying to seem genuinely interested.

"Yeah?" He turned to the rows of seating and held out an arm. "Well, have a seat anywhere—"

"Oh my god!" Lena shrieked as she skidded to a stop in front of me. "I just saw a clown pissing on the side of the building. What in the hell have you gotten us into? I swear if I catch something from being here, you're paying my doctor bill." She finally noticed Trevor behind me. "Well, *hello*."

He held out his hand. "The name's Trevor Steele."

"Of course it is." Her cheeks blushed a little as he took her hand in his. "Lena Davis."

"We're going to find a seat," I said. Grabbing Lena's arm, I pulled her toward me.

"I wouldn't sit in the front row," he warned.

"Don't think we can handle it?" I felt more confident with my best friend at my side.

"Oh, I'm sure you can handle it." He winked. "But Payne's fans are crazy." His left eyebrow rose just a hair, as if hiding an inside joke.

"Noted."

"Later, ladies." His grin told me he definitely knew something we didn't.

Two fights, a plate full of BBQ nachos, and two beers later, the lights went out. I opened my eyes wider, trying to make out the shadows in the dark. The roar of the crowd startled me, causing me to reach out for Lena's arm. The excitement in the air had us rising to our feet, joining the rest of the audience.

The crowd quieted as the overhead speakers came on. I waited, thinking heavy metal was about to blare through the room, but I only heard footsteps. Loud crackles and pops surrounded the stillness of the room. It reminded me of when I used to go to my grandma's house on the lake, and she'd play old records.

After a couple of seconds, a man walked up to the cage, and the crowd lost it. They chanted, "Payne! Payne! Payne!" Each time, growing louder and more frenzied.

Lena leaned over and yelled over the din of the crowd, "Shit just got real."

She was right; the excitement in the air was palpable. This fight must've been the highlight of the night. I'd only taken two paragraphs of notes through the first two fights. And that included the intoxicated middle-aged lady in the front row who flashed everyone for a free beer.

I stood, patiently waiting for the fighter to reveal himself in the lights over the cage. With all the commotion in the stands, I assumed he'd play up to his fans in the over-crowded gym. He didn't. His silhouette, tall and muscular, stood stalk-still just outside the cage; his stare straight ahead, waiting for the go-ahead. He had on nothing but a pair of blue shorts, and his tan skin sucked me in like a vacuum. I licked my lips, my gaze focused on his abs. Each one was perfectly shaped, making me wonder how long it took him to get them like that.

His right hand flinched, drawing my gaze away from his stomach. As calm as his demeanor was, that one small movement made me think he was nervous, or maybe just eager to get started. His head made one slight movement to the right, and mine followed. Trevor sat in a metal folding chair in the corner. He nodded once, as if giving him advice without words.

Payne walked to the center of the cage, not acknowledging the moment that had passed between the two. Looking back and forth between them both, I noticed Trevor was much more relaxed. I didn't know if this was due to his laid-back personality, or if he was just that confident in Payne's abilities. Payne's dark eyes narrowed, seemingly annoyed with the delay of getting down to business.

Hypnotized, I didn't look away from him, even when the other fighter entered the cage. It wasn't until the lady in front of us startled me that I looked away.

"Kick his ass, Payne!" she screamed, holding a poster that read *I'm a Sucker for Payne*. Underneath, was an arrow pointing downward, so that it pointed at her when she held it above her head.

Payne stood with his shoulders back in confidence, perfectly centered in the cage, not once looking out into the crowd. He didn't respond to the support they gave him. Instead, he narrowed in on his opponent, eyes laser focused. I couldn't imagine what the other guy was thinking. Hell, *I* was intimidated by Payne at forty feet away. The tension reached new heights, almost percolating around the two fighters. As I took in the fans, it was easy to see I wasn't the only one amazed.

Both fighters circled each other slowly. Their eyes fixated solely on each other, their fists punching the air like a warm-up. Lopez moved his bare feet around quickly, which made me think he had more energy. I gasped when he brought his right foot up to kick Payne in the ribs. Payne blocked it and smiled.

I let out a breath I hadn't realized I was holding. Tension gathered in my shoulders, causing heat to radiate from my muscles. Curiosity ignited deep in my gut.

I'd almost forgotten the reason I was there. I needed to get the feeling of the place down on paper, so I didn't forget. The certainty that one of the athletes would be taking a loss intrigued me.

Lopez kicked him in the thigh, then quickly punched Payne in the face. I watched, surprised that he'd gotten one in on him without so much as a block from Payne. Not like the first time, when he'd tried the same kick.

"Why didn't he block that one?" I shouted toward Lena, but her answer was drowned out by a sudden crescendo of voices around us.

I bent down to grab my pen and paper, while balancing my third beer. Whatever happened next, it needed to be documented. Now that I'd witnessed the atmosphere, I was eager to pen the experience. At another roar from the crowd, Lena bounced on her heels, emulating the rest of the audience. It startled me, causing me to slosh some of my beer on the person in front of me.

"I'm so sorry—" I started to say, until a giant fist swung at me so fast, I froze. As her fist connected with my cheek, I fell back into my seat and rattled the row of chairs.

The larger lady leaned over me and said, "That's your warning."

Lena still hadn't noticed I'd been assaulted, and continued her whistling and clapping, as if she were a life-long supporter of the sport.

Dazed, I shook my head, attempting to gather my thoughts.

I've just been punched. In the face.

I moved my jaw back and forth, almost stunned that it didn't hurt more. Even with my not-so-pure past, black eyes had never been a part of it. I imagined blood running down my face and a dark-purple bruise forming, when Lena finally looked down at me.

"Willow, you just missed the coolest thing I've ever seen! That guy just lunged in the air and punched the other guy's lights out. Oh my

God. We are *so* coming back!" Her eyebrows furrowed in confusion as she took in my appearance. "What's wrong with you?"

I waved a hand toward the body blocking my view. "That lady just hit me!"

Lena's horrified expression would have made me laugh in any other circumstance. "Who?" she mouthed, because the crowd was still going crazy.

"Her," I said and pointed at the brute of a woman. "I spilled my beer on her accidently and she knocked me on my ass."

"Hey!" Lena shouted at the back of the woman's head. "You can't just punch my friend and think you'll get away with it."

The woman turned to her friend and said, "Hold my beer." She then leaned toward me and Lena, making us both sink back into our chairs. "Want to bet?" Her sausage fingers gripped the back of her chair so tight, her knuckles turned white. "She caused me to miss more than half of Payne's match."

"It only lasted thirty seconds before he knocked that guy out." Lena huffed.

"Boy, she's a smart one." She and her hillbilly friend laughed.

As if she'd suddenly realized we were the ones out of place, Lena nudged my shoulder. "Let's get out of here. She's wearing a flannel with the arms cut out." One side of her mouth turned downward, and her eyes widened.

After grabbing my bag, we hastily made our escape.

"Sorry you didn't get to see much grappling tonight." Trevor's voice carried from behind us.

"Yeah, maybe next time," I called over my shoulder. I tried to smile, grimacing from the contusion I was positive was already forming.

"I'm sure I could talk Payne into some sparring later this week. I feel bad for taking your money and you didn't get to see any grappling. Come by. We'll hook you up."

"Sounds good."

A tug in my lower abdomen forced me to look back toward the cage. Payne's gaze trapped me, causing a small sigh to escape my lips. Like a calm after the storm, the noise from the crowd faded away, as if he and I were the only two in the room. He'd just won a fight, and I wondered why he was still standing in the cage by himself.

With my hand on Lena's shoulder, I turned back to our exit and walked forward, while she forged a path. The whole time I walked away from him, it felt wrong. It was as if I should have run back to him, even though I had no idea why. I pushed the foreign instinct down and continued to follow the crowd out of the gym.

As bodies pushed and pulled around us, I kept my hand securely in Lena's, hoping to get out without another injury. With Payne's win, it was as if the whole crowd had won; all of them with more vigor than they knew what to do with. Upon exiting the building, I breathed in the night air, completely shocked at what I'd just experienced.

Lord, what had Andy gotten me into? At least I had more than enough material for an exceptional story. That was a plus, and Andy would be pleased.

CHAPTER 3
CONNER

I JUMPED off the side of the cage, refusing to regard the mob that had formed after the match. I made my way down the path to the extended hallway, bypassing the announcer and local television crew who reported on the fights every week. I didn't give two shits about talking to someone on camera. They could keep the fame.

With each step I took, the announcer's voice trailed further behind me, as he tried to rally the horde for a cash drawing they were having. They were still calling my name when I entered the locker room. My head pounded, probably more from the adrenaline dump than the actual fighting. I quickly threw my sweatpants on, along with my socks and sneakers. I hadn't even cleaned my bloody hands or face before I slid out the backdoor, on my way to my truck.

Screw them. Screw everyone. Too many emotions were shooting through my body at once. Anger, pride, self-doubt, fear . . . I had no idea how accomplishing a goal could make me feel so lost.

On my drive home from another win, my mind raced. I knew I was thinking way in advance, but if I did ever go pro, eventually the public would find out about my past. And that was something I didn't want dug back up.

After my sentence had been handed down, I'd never forgotten the look in my mother's eyes. Like a wild animal caught in a hunter's trap, she'd wailed once, then quickly closed her mouth. I'd choked back my own tears at the apparent internal struggle she'd fought to keep her emotions from escaping.

She'd become small, like she was shrinking right before my eyes, as she walked over to the victim's family. I'd never forget her next words. "I feel sick. So sick, I can't even look at him. My heart is broken and will never mend."

I watched the exchange, along with the rest of the court room, waiting for the mother of the victim to respond. It was gut-wrenching. Two mothers—both of their hearts laid bare for the entire world to see.

The boy's mother looked like an empty shell. Like her skin and bones were the only thing holding her up. Her eyes grew in surprise that my mom had approached her. She stayed silent as her family members led her out of the court room. Standing behind my mother in handcuffs, I knew I was the reason for her pain. I'd broken her. I'd broken her spirit, and she'd broken mine with that one sentence. Those words were the last I'd heard from her.

Clearing a green light, only minutes from my home, my thoughts switched to the dark-haired beauty from the fight. Her hair had flowed effortlessly in soft curls down to the middle of her back. And the black pants she'd worn had fit her like a glove. We'd shared a moment, almost as if my thoughts were linked to hers by magic. Her eyes had been drawn straight to mine.

The clatter of my keys being thrown into the bowl by my front door rang out in the small space. I flicked the lights on in the hallway and leaned against the wall. With nowhere to go, or no one to keep me occupied, the buzz from the fight wore off.

Thump. Thump. Thump.

The back of my head bounced off the wall, in sync with my heart-beat. The sound grew faster and louder with each passing second. I turned my head back to the small table in the entryway. The keys to my pickup glinted in the light. *It is less than a five-minute ride to the liquor store.*

I ran my hands through my hair and tugged hard once I reached the ends. I popped my knuckles, knowing I had to do something with the extreme urge to fuck up my life.

The phone in my pocket weighed my pants down on the right side, just a hair. I shivered, and goose bumps settled on the patch of exposed skin between my T-shirt and sweats. *Simone would feel good.* I could burn a couple of hours with her, then hopefully crash.

Making my way to the shower, I adjusted the temperature of the water and made up my mind. At least it would ease the tension in my body. I quickly undressed and leaned on the vanity, bringing my face less than an inch from the mirror. Searching my own eyes for answers, I eventually closed them, with no newfound resolution. One vice wasn't any better than the other—I knew that—but one reminded me of who I was, and the other made me forget about it all. At least for a little while.

Conner: Come over.
Simone: On my way.

I clicked off my phone and stepped under the scorching spray.

I needed to talk to Rick. I wasn't even sure what my purse was from the fight. I hadn't cared, to be honest. It would be peanuts to what Steele made in the pro league, but money was money. Steele had always been aware that Rick paid us for our fights, but kept his nose clean where that was concerned. He could be suspended for illegal betting, and he'd told me once before that no one was worth his career in the pro league. I believed him, which is why I rarely spoke about my pay days with him.

I rotated my shoulders, along with my head, allowing the water to rush over me. The tightness from my neck, up to the back of my head, bloomed into a full-blown headache. The rust-colored water circled the drain and left me numb. I scrubbed as hard as I could. As if the pressure might erase the punches I'd taken, only an hour before.

Bodily pain was no hardship for me. Even as a kid, I could break a bone, slice my hand open, or even fall off the roof, and I never cried. I'd always been physically tough. Why that couldn't carry over to my mental state, I'd never know. Hence my internal struggle between drinking my cares away and calling on a semi-good lay.

Stepping out of the shower, I ran a towel over my head. I chuckled at myself, for feeling like I was taking one for the team. A win for my body was a loss for the alcohol. At least there was a plus to one of the outcomes. My doorbell rang. I tossed the towel in the hamper and strolled to the door, ready to release the pent-up energy I'd created in the shower.

"How was your fight?" She smiled, eyes moving down my body, landing on my junk.

"Fine." I stepped aside, allowing her to come inside.

"I'm assuming you—" Her words were cut off as she squealed when I threw her over my shoulder. "Conner!" She giggled.

I carried her into my bedroom and dropped her on the bed. Kissing her shoulder, I pulled off her shirt. My body buzzed with anticipation, clearing my mind. I was thankful there was zero thinking involved in finding my release.

Her hand pushed at my chest. "Conner."

"What?" I snapped.

Her smile disappeared, and she cocked her head to the side, challenging me.

I hung my head and blew out a frustrated breath. "Look, I'm tired, I'm sore, and I have a killer headache. This was a mistake." I should have known a decision made in haste wouldn't have worked out.

If looks could kill, I'd have dropped like a sack of potatoes. Her eyelids squinted until they were mere slits.

I placed my right hand over my junk and stood up. "What?" I was over the whole thing already.

She propped herself up on her elbows, but made no sign of getting off my bed.

I glanced around, making a show, as if to tell her I wasn't following why she wasn't leaving. "Did you hear me?"

She rose, taking small steps until she stood facing me. I could see the wheels in her head turning, so I waited for her next move. Her bare breasts hit my chest softly. Then her hardened nipples pressed into me so firm, her round globes flattened like pancakes. Neither of us moved to wrap our arms around each other, nor did my body rise to her challenge.

"What are you doing?"

"You're an asshole." Her raspy voice was so low, I had to concentrate on listening to her. "The worst kind too. Because, at the end of the day, even though you squeeze out a couple of nice words here and there, it really is all about you. Every fucking thing. The fights. Your vendetta against mankind. Your family, or lack thereof—"

"Get out," I said through clenched teeth. "Get your shit, and don't come back."

"You're the sorriest lay I've ever had, Conner. I've never met anyone more selfish. Have a nice life, fighting in the *amateur* league." She huffed as she picked up her shirt and stormed out of the bedroom.

I got back in bed, proving the point that I was perfectly fine with her leaving. If she'd been a dude, I would have punched her in the throat for even thinking she knew anything about my family. Placing my hands behind my head, I squeezed my eyes shut, wishing the last twenty minutes hadn't happened.

Tuesday couldn't come fast enough. My next fight, Michael Sullins, had drawn the short straw. Funny how my mind immediately went to thrashing someone. Adrenaline pulsed through my body, and my insides tingled at the impulse. I rolled over, settling in for a miserable night. My thoughts would keep my mind busy, and even if I was lucky enough to find sleep, my nightmares would wake me up. It was my routine—my fucking life.

Groggy, my ears perked from the sound of my phone buzzing, causing vibrations against the nightstand. I slapped the wood with my eyes still closed. After two tries, my hand landed on my phone.

I glanced at my clock to see it was only seven o'clock in the morning. "Yeah?"

"Man, Gregory's over here talking shit. Saying you'll never gain a match with him, and that—"

I didn't hear any more because I ended the call.

Gregory had been talking shit since I'd beaten his cousin Kramer. If it had been up to me, I would have fought his ass first. I knew I could take him—even without much experience—but Steele wanted me to get my feet wet first. I didn't much care about the order of opponents. I got in the cage with whoever he matched me up with, and would continue to do so until Frank Fuller, the CEO of the AFL decided to offer me a contract.

With that being said, I wasn't going to let that son-of-a-bitch talk smack about me in my own gym. I pulled my sweats on in one swift move. Shoving my bare feet into my sneakers, I brushed my teeth in record time and started for the gym.

Steele met me at the door and placed a hand on my shoulder. "He's gone."

I looked around, taking in the other fighters watching me. They were curious. They'd obviously been witness to Gregory talking shit. I nodded, and followed Steele back to his office. I took a seat and slid my hat low on my forehead, until the shadow of the brim hid my eyes.

"He's just trying to get in your head." Steel crossed his arms, leaning against the edge of his desk.

I crossed mine too. "He's pissing me off."

"Then I guess his plan is working." He rounded the desk to take a seat behind it.

I flipped my hat backward and placed my arms on my knees. I knew what he was saying. My temper was getting in the way of my professionalism. "I get it, okay?"

"Do you?" His eyes were pinned on mine. "Conner, you are one of the most talented fighters I've ever had the honor to train with. I saw something in you the first time you ever walked into my gym." I kept quiet, allowing him to go on. "You have the potential to rule this sport, but you can't let your demons get in the way. I know you carry a burden, but if you want any kind of future for yourself, you're going to have to find somewhere else to put it."

"So, you're telling me, if some fuckface was talking shit about you, you'd turn the other cheek?" I asked, knowing he wouldn't.

"No. I'd settle it in the cage. Which is what you need to do." He rounded his desk and leaned on it, directly in front of me. "You reacted exactly how I thought you would though, rushing over here, ready to kick some ass. But remember this . . . the first rule in this sport is to not take anything personal. This is your *job*. It's no different than a thug fighting the police. The thug is fighting the badge, not the man who wears it. Gregory sees you as a threat. He's been trying to go pro for two years. You are the obstacle standing in his way. The suits are going to put their money in one man. One."

I took a moment to let his words sink in. I wanted to shred Gregory. I could still feel my blood boiling, but I stayed silent, my thoughts somewhere between violent rage and complete peace. I knew Steele was only trying to help me.

I leaned back in the chair and pushed my emotions down deep. The bottom line was, I needed a pay check. I could either let this work for me—this fighting thing that had basically fallen in my lap—or I could go hammer two-by-fours together for cash that probably wouldn't pay my rent.

I blew out a breath and bounced my knee. "I get it. I want a career. One I can be proud of."

"Do you, brother?"

"Brother?" I asked. "Is that where we are?"

He nodded. "That's where we are."

I stood, eye level with him at an even six-foot-two. We shook hands, and I slapped his shoulder. I appreciated what he was doing. He'd proven himself to me. He had my back.

"Let's get out there, so I can kick your ass," he said.

I chuckled as we exited his office. "In your dreams. I'm still pissed."

I rounded the corner and noticed the beautiful brunette who'd been at my last fight, standing at the front counter, dressed like she was having dinner at the White House.

Steele walked around me and greeted her. "Willow, right?"

She held her hand out, all business. "Yes. So nice to see you again, Trevor."

Trevor? So, the cocksucker knows her.

"Are you taking me up on my offer?" Trevor asked.

What kind of offer?

"I am. I'd also like to set up a couple of interviews for the paper." She held up the media badge hanging from her neck. "If any of your guys are willing, that is."

No way in hell I'm doing an interview.

I made my way over to warm up. She was obviously there for business. No sense in me sticking around for something I was not willing

29

to be a part of. Grabbing the handles on the jump rope, I closed my eyes and started a slow and steady rhythm, counting each jump in my head.

Something swirled around my gut, pulling and tugging, until I gave in and opened my eyes. With her back to me, I couldn't help but stare. Black, sleek heels graced her feet. The red slacks she had on fit her trim body, showing off her hour-glass figure. I pictured both my hands wrapped around her small, belted waist. My fingertips would touch, no doubt. If I slid them down, I'd have two handfuls . . .

I tightened my grip and sped up, closing my eyes once again. Damn, this would be the day I forgot my iPod. I inhaled through my nostrils and blew the warm breaths out my mouth. Prison had taught me a few things in a fucked-up kind of way. I just needed to get back to that place mentally, where nothing touched me. Nothing affected me.

I didn't waste any more time thinking impure thoughts about the beautiful woman Steele was still talking to at the front desk. I focused instead on preparing myself for my daily spar.

After jumping, I stretched again, and finished up with a round of tossing a medicine ball. Placing my headgear on, I looked up to see Steele and the woman approaching me.

"Conner. This is Willow Stevens. She's a reporter—"

"No," I interrupted him. Her eyes darted to mine and her smile fell. I hadn't meant to offend her. "Sorry, I uh . . . don't do interviews."

"Do you mind me asking why?" She cocked her head to the side, appearing genuinely curious.

Knowing I'd never divulge the constant turmoil I swam in, I kept my answer short. "Just don't."

"Let's go, Payne," Johnny said. He stood at the entrance of the cage, waving me over.

Placing my mouth guard in, I stepped in without looking back at her.

Willow took a seat in a chair just to the right of the cage. It was the best seat in the house, but not for positive reasons. We'd designated it the Little Bitch chair, for fighters who let women bust their concentration. It didn't matter if they denied being whipped. Majority ruled in the gym. So instead of working out and training, the dude on the carpet would have to sit in the purple chair like a little bitch, while watching the rest of us train.

I tried to block Willow out of my mind as I went three rounds with Tommy. The irony of it almost had me rolling my eyes. As hard as I tried, I was aware of her to my right, watching us in awe. Her facial expressions were a mixture of shock and complete infatuation. The look was not lust, but interest in our movements. Every punch, every kick, I'd hear her breath catch. I tried not to lose my concentration, and went extra hard at him for the simple fact that I was sidetracked.

I hated it.

I couldn't give two shits about anyone on the outside, so the fact that she was taking over my thoughts annoyed me. I didn't want to think about how the top two buttons on her blouse were unbuttoned, or that her damn red pants were so tight, I could see her thigh muscles and bare ankles. And I sure as fuck didn't want to be turned on by those stupid black high heels that seemed to get higher each time I glanced over at her.

The angrier I got, the harder I hit. Finally, Tommy pushed me back and told me he was done. Seeing his confusion pissed me off even more. We were supposed to have just been sparring, yet I'd gone at him full speed. I spit my mouth piece out and jumped out of the cage, not offering him an explanation.

As I grabbed my bag, I heard her ask Tommy if he'd be willing to do an interview. He said yes, the jackass. I wiped my face with my T-shirt and casually glanced at them as they took a seat in the bleachers. Her long hair moved in sync with her body, and she tucked a lock behind her ear as she started taking notes.

I tilted my water bottle up, taking two long swigs, but my eyes never left her. I wasn't sure what it was, but the knot in my throat threatened to stop the liquid from going down. It could have been that I felt like holding my breath to the point of feeling light-headed, or exhaling so long I gave myself a buzz at just the sight of her. I had never been so thrown off at the sight of a woman the way I was with her, and I didn't even know her. But I wanted to.

CHAPTER 4
WILLOW

"HONEY, do you mind if Bob and I stop by?" My mom, newly in love, couldn't keep the sweetness out of her voice.

"Of course not. Make it six, and I'll cook."

"I'll bring something. We have news," she said.

I smiled, surprised they'd waited this long. "Okay, I'll see you then." Glancing at my office door, I took in a battered-looking Andy as I ended my phone call.

"What are we so smiley about?" he asked.

"Oh, just my mom. Bob proposed."

"Joy." He grunted, taking a seat.

"Are you all right?" I'd been concerned for some time, but he was my boss and I wouldn't cross the line. He'd never been one for getting too personal, and I respected that. But for a few weeks now, he'd been showing up to work hungover, untidy, and in a foul mood. I hadn't wanted to approach him for anything.

He blew out a deep breath before he spoke. "Carmen left me."

"I'm sorry. I hadn't realized you were having trouble."

"No trouble. Just her cheating on me."

Not to mention your gambling problem. I stood and walked over to him. "I'm sorry she treated you that way." I patted his shoulder, not knowing what else to do, or why he'd confided in me.

His head tilted to the side, examining my touch. "Willow, I know—"

"Andy, can you check the downtown music piece?" Chelsea interrupted, coming to a halt in the doorway. "I've got half an hour until I have to go to the gala." The intern's eyes shot to my hand on his shoulder.

I pulled my hand back quickly, which only made me look guilty. Her eyes widened, and I grimaced. Crossing my arms, I tucked my hands tightly into fists, realizing she'd gotten the wrong idea.

"Yeah, I'll be right there." He stood and nodded. "Thanks, Willow."

"You're welcome. If there's anything I can do, let me know."

He nodded and trailed behind Chelsea.

After Andy confessed his troubles, I chose to remain at my desk for the rest of the afternoon. I hated that his life seemed full of chaos, but at the same time, I could tell he was making personal choices that were probably contributing to it. Every few minutes, I found myself glancing at the clock on the wall, praying an hour had passed. And every single time, it had been no more than twenty minutes. Frustrated with the whole situation, I packed up my belongings at four-thirty, willing to risk slipping out, hoping no one would notice.

My stop at the grocery store took no more than ten minutes. Uneasiness set firm in my gut, as I grabbed both grocery bags from my car, and headed inside to start dinner. The last thing I wanted or needed was unnecessary drama in my workplace.

Still in a funk, I barely heard my mom as she settled into her place at the bar. "Did you hear me, honey?" The stool scraping across my tile floor startled me.

"Oh, I'm sorry." I stirred the sauce, giving her my full attention.

"Are you okay? Have a rough day at work?"

"Something like that," I chose to say, instead of what I was thinking. *I'm pretty sure my boss is using, because as much as I hate to admit it, my past experience allows me to recognize the signs.*

"Let me finish this, okay? Go take a load off. I'll meet you in the dining room." She slipped past me and pulled the utensil out of my hand, before shooing me away.

"Thanks, Mom." I grabbed my wine, and joined Bob in the dining room.

He smiled as I took a seat across from him, then got right to the point. "Just so you know, I love your mother very much. I know it seems fast, but I don't want to waste any more time. We're not getting any younger." His hands were clasped together, resting on the table.

"I appreciate that, Bob. I just want her happy."

"I plan on spending everyday making that happen." He grinned again, wider this time. It was clear by the relaxation in his shoulders, he was relieved by my response.

"What are you going to make happen?" Mom asked, bringing the pasta to the table.

"I was just telling Willow that I plan on making you happy every day."

She kissed his forehead and took a seat beside him. "I'm very happy, dear. You both make me happy." She looked to me. "And you're okay with everything?" Mom held her left hand in the air to show off her ring.

"Of course. I love you." I took another sip of my wine. "Sorry if I've been distracted; work is nuts right now." I reached for her hand. "Tell me all about how you guys plan to celebrate."

I focused on her the rest of the dinner, making sure to talk nothing but wedding and honeymoon plans. I listened as she and Bob told me every small detail they'd already decided on, and the larger ones she expected my help with.

At eight o'clock, they left hand in hand, but only after my mother cleaned every square inch of my kitchen. I knew better than to argue, so I humored her. Turning off the lights, I headed straight for my bed. I wasn't even tired. I'd surpassed that long ago. I was worn out.

Sinking into my pillow, I closed my eyes. A smile spread across my face as a rogue thought of Conner Payne came to me. His tough exterior and no-nonsense disposition probably scared a lot of people away, but not me. Curiosity rolled through my mind a mile a minute. Questions, probabilities, and genuine interest circled my gut like the wings of a hummingbird.

Then thoughts of Andy invaded my Conner daydream. I rolled

over, pulling the blankets up over my head. I despised that I had once been where he was. His blatant disregard for his well-being, his career, or anything else for that matter, made me feel sorry for him because I saw his reckless abandonment for what it was—total and complete hopelessness. I had known that feeling all too well.

Lena nudged my shoulder as we entered the club. "I can't believe you took Tommy up on his offer."

"Stop saying it's a date." I rolled my eyes. "He casually mentioned that he'd be out, and asked if we wanted to stop by and hang out. That's all."

"I never said it was a date."

"I know you're thinking it. So, shut up." I poked her in the chest, and she laughed, trying to dodge the contact as we approached the doorman.

The club was packed, and the bar was three deep. "I don't think we'll be able to find a table," I said, side-stepping bodies at every turn.

"Doesn't look like we'll need one." Lena pointed to the VIP area, just one floor up. Tommy and his friends were sitting on a red velvet couch, waving for us to join them. I nodded and took Lena's outstretched hand to follow her lead.

Tommy was waiting on us at the top of the stairs. "Hey, ladies. Welcome to my party." His boyish grin gave away the few drinks in his system. I leaned in for a quick hug before he led us to the couch, where the rest of his group were hanging out. "Guys, this is Willow and her friend, Lena. I think some of you may have done an interview with her the other day."

I recognized a couple of the guys as they nodded and raised their drinks in my direction. It was rowdy—to be expected—but controlled as well. We were the only women in the area, which surprised me. After exchanging pleasantries with one of Tommy's buddies, I glanced to my right. Conner Payne stared back at me, as though we were the only two people in the room.

I glanced down, feeling embarrassingly explored. As if his

cognizance was all he needed to discover my cloaked character. Without speaking a word to me, his silence spoke volumes. He saw something in me. I swallowed, wondering what it was.

My mind was strong. The outer wall of self-preservation that therapy had provided over the years had given me a mental armor no one had been able to penetrate, including Lena. Until that very moment, when he looked through me, as if he was able to gauge my moral compass.

Even in a crowd, seated with people to either side of him, he had a loneliness about him. Seemingly out of place, even though he appeared chill. Conversations rolled on around him, but not once did he join in. The black T-shirt he wore stretched tight across his chest as he leaned back into the couch, his right arm resting comfortably on the back cushions. Long legs stretched out before him; his left hand relaxed on his thigh. His mood to anyone else may have come off as bored at best, but the tension pulsating between us shook my insides like an earthquake, and I was confident he had the same feeling. His gaze held mine as the drinks were being poured and laughter bellowed around us.

I moved to sit down with Lena and Tommy, giving Payne my back.

"How long have you worked at the paper?" Tommy asked as Conner's silence beat against my back in perfect time with the slow, soulful music.

I smiled, but it felt fake. "Two years."

"Cool. I'd be fine with more interviews, if you ever need someone to fill a column."

"I appreciate that." My skin burned, tiny bursts of heat spreading, as if a tattoo gun repeatedly punctured my sensitive skin. His stillness created an atmosphere where my senses were in overdrive. "I may take you up on that. It seems I've missed out on some juicy stories by not covering you guys before."

"Oh, we got juicy." Tommy smirked. "We'll knock the socks off your readers. Plus, it will help us out too. Most of us are trying to make it to the AFL."

"AFL?" I sipped my wine, genuinely interested in the direction our conversation was going. Last week, I hadn't even known the league existed, and now I was trying to get the inside scoop. I blamed it on the reporter in me.

"American Fighting League. Trevor Steele, you know the owner of the gym we were at the other night? He fights in it. It's a pro league."

"Oh. So why does he have amateur fights in his personal gym?" I was almost as curious about Steele as I was about Conner Payne.

"He's just cool like that," Tommy replied. "Steele helps all of us out. He lets us train and fight at his gym, and certain fights attract the AFL owner. He has the connections."

I nodded, agreeing with him that Steele was cool. Helping the other guys out like that was indeed a nice thing to do, especially knowing he didn't benefit from it.

"I'm heading out." Conner interrupted our conversation to give Tommy a tap on the shoulder.

"Come on, man. It's still early," Tommy said.

Conner shook his head. "I got shit to do." He made it seem effort-less; walking away.

Tommy nodded. "You working-out tomorrow?"

I couldn't help but stare at him, waiting for another word from those lips. He glanced at the rest of the group, then back at Tommy. "Don't know yet. Catch you later."

After his brief goodbye, Conner looked over his shoulder, making our final connection of the night. I'd never taken my eyes from him, even though Lena and the others were laughing hysterically at some-thing one of them had said.

He stuffed his hands in his pockets, while I uncrossed my bare legs. His gaze flickered down at the movement, the hunger in his eyes taking my breath away. My lips parted just as he looked back up at me. My lungs expanded, making my dress tight enough to bust at the seams. I carefully let the air out, managing to release it without feeling lightheaded. He quickly turned for the exit, ending the moment.

Watching his back move through the crowd, I wondered what it was about him that made me feel like I knew him. Not in an acquain-tance sort of way. And not in a seen-him-before sort of way. I'm talking about recognizing the inside parts of another human being, and relating with them on a level that scratches the surface of intimacy.

"Want to dance?" One of Tommy's friends asked, interrupting my one-sided staring contest.

I took one last sip of my wine and closed my eyes, taking a moment to gather my thoughts before I answered him. My limbs were heavy; my body, lethargic. I shook it off the best I could and opened my eyes, focusing on Gage.

A boyish grin spread across his face as I grabbed his hand, and he winked at my acceptance. It seemed he didn't have a care in the world, and honestly, after the encounter I'd just had with Conner, I welcomed easy.

Gage turned me around, then dipped me—almost dropping me— and we both laughed as I clung to him. There was something intriguing about him. His dark hair curled on the sides because of sweat. He looked like a young child instead of someone who kicked people's asses for a living.

"What made you want to be a journalist?" he asked.

"I don't know." I raised my voice loud enough for him to hear me over the music. "I guess I felt like I had something to say. I usually don't cover sports, but the guy who does is sick. And my boss sort of pushed me out into this world."

"You like it. I can see it in your eyes!" He grinned, twirling me around. "You're surprised that us assholes are entertaining."

"Honestly? Yes. I love the excitement." I smiled, matching his. "To think that all of you guys are working your asses off to go pro is fun to watch. Hard work and intensity? I can get behind that."

"Helps that we're all hot as hell too, yeah?" He laughed this time.

"Right . . . that is exactly what I was thinking." I rolled my eyes, and held my smile in. He wasn't wrong.

"Willow!" I turned to see Lena heading our way. "Potty break. Sorry, Gage. I need to steal her for a minute."

"I'll be around," he said, but didn't look at either of us. His gaze had already moved on to a sexy brunette who'd been dancing next to us with her friend.

"What's up?" I tried to ask, but she was already dragging me into the bathroom.

"I cannot believe you left me with that fucking geezer!" She shrieked. "He reached in front of me and grazed my boob. His sixty-five-year-old ass touched my tit." She grabbed two handfuls and bounced her boobs. "I think it deflated! It's seriously smaller than the other one now. It shriveled up!"

I chuckled, turning her around so I could inspect them. After grabbing them, I assured her they were both the same size. "What sixty-five-year-old?"

"Some agent they knew." She turned to the mirror, and reached into her bra, giving both breasts a lift in the cups. I giggled at the sight of her inspecting each one. "He barged in at our table, drunk as a skunk, and set his sights on me."

"Gross."

"That's not why we have to leave though." She bit her lip.

I knew every time Lena brought up getting the hell out of dodge, when we were not ready to leave, meant that she had done something. Something stupid. I rolled my eyes, then faced her head on, so she could explain the situation.

She took my hands in hers, as if asking my forgiveness, before she admitted her wrongdoing. "It's not my fault."

"Go on," I urged.

"He kept inching closer to me. Looking down my shirt when the other guys weren't looking. Accidently hitting my boobs. Whispering stupid shit in my ear. I'd had enough, Willow. So, when I got up to come get you, I climbed over him because I knew he'd love it."

"Okay . . . then why are we leaving without telling anyone bye?" I knew that wasn't the end of it.

"I may have crunched his balls with the pointy end of my stiletto."

My eyes bulged. "You stuck your heel in his dick?"

"By my calculations, I put extra pressure on his nut sack, right at the bottom. I didn't actually get the ball, though. Only the extra skin." She pulled her hand from mine to demonstrate with her thumb and index finger.

"You tried to find his nut sack while all this was going on?"

"Hell yeah I did. I was going to make it count. But now I think we need to go, because he was bent over, talking about needing to puke.

And I saw Steele scooting around the table to help him. So, needless to say, I don't think we're welcomed in the VIP area anymore."

"I can't take you anywhere." I shook my head, grinning at my best friend.

"I'll make it up to you, I promise. Just not tonight. I can't have Grandpa hobbling after me all night, fucking up my game."

Exiting the bathroom, we glanced around the bar to make sure no one was looking for us as we slid out. The last thing I wanted was to have Steele revoking my invitation to the gym. I'd gotten more material from the fighters than I had in a month of working on feminism.

CHAPTER 5
CONNER

AS I ROLLED up to the stop sign, a small neon light perched on the roof of an older building caught my attention. Perfect. The whole-in-the-wall bar was small, dark, and probably dingy. I wanted to drive past it, to forget about this tradition, but my gut turned at the thought of me leaving it behind. Something inside me wouldn't allow it.

Giving in, I parked on the east side of the building. Bright colored graffiti covered the exposed brick. The clearest message read: *If you're drinking to forget, please pay in advance.*

Placing my keys in my pocket, I took in the nearly vacant parking lot—only three other vehicles accompanied my own. Each step I took toward the front door felt odd, like I'd somehow forgotten the simple task of placing one foot in front of the other.

The dark room pulsed with the mournful wail of an electric guitar. Faces wrapped in shadows turned toward me. Their features were blurred by a smoky haze. The old tickle started in my throat, but I forced it back down with a hard swallow. I took a seat on the last stool at the bar closest to the wall. I didn't even take my jacket off, knowing I wasn't there to wind down; and no amount of freedom would help relax me.

"What can I get you?" The older man had gray hair pulled back into a ponytail. He tapped the bar, but did it without a smile. Probably the owner, and probably over drunks. I tried twice before I was able to reply. I despised myself in that moment.

A couple of minutes later, he slid my order in front of me. I nodded my thanks, not making eye contact. I stared at the lowball glass the whiskey was in. There were two water spots around the rim, and a speck of something black at the bottom that I'd only been able to see once I picked the drink up and swirled it around. It smelled like heaven.

If I fall off the wagon, I can get back on tomorrow.

"You're over thinking it."

I glanced up, annoyed that someone had interrupted my internal battle. My anger subsided upon seeing Willow's smile. "You think so?"

"I do." She nodded.

"What makes you think you know anything about me?" As soon as the words left my mouth, I frowned. Reaching around her, my whiskers almost touching her hip, I pulled a wooden stool up for her. An apology. Sort of.

"I've seen this before. Been there a few times myself," she said. Her knee pressed into my thigh as she mounted the stool I'd just offered. The air that surrounded us took on a new feel. The thickness of the atmosphere pressed into me, almost weighing me down. Tightness gathered in my chest; the sting from her touch ignited a reaction in me that I wasn't sure what to do with. With her right heel propped on the bottom of the stool, her knee bumped my thigh again. But this time, she didn't move it. I didn't pull back either.

I circled my index finger around the rim of the glass. Around and around it went. I focused on the slow rhythm, but I could see her out of the corner of my eye. She never looked away, even when I scowled.

"All right," I finally said. "You told me how you recognize it. But tell me *why* you recognize it." It was then I looked up at her. The blue in her eyes damn near swallowed me whole.

A soft sigh escaped her lips. "Are we spilling secrets here, Payne?"

"Didn't say a word about secrets." My gaze held hers, not a breath passing between either of us. The intensity we shared at the mention of secrets held me in my place.

"You don't strike me as the type to pinky promise."

I bit down on the inside of my cheek to stop the urge to grin at her change in topic. "What the fuck is that?"

"A pinky promise is more sacred than a regular promise," she said. "You know, people break promises all the time. But pinky promises, those can't ever be broken. The person you promised will drop dead if you break it." Her eyes widened, and a grin spread wide across her face as she tried to convince me.

"Want to test your theory?" I rested my chin on my shoulder. "Live on the wild side for a bit?"

She gasped. "How could you be so careless? This is the *truth*. My mom told me when I was six years old, and I've never broken one." She leaned into my personal space, just enough for me to catch a whiff of her floral perfume.

"Hmm." I hadn't meant to release the grunt out loud. I also wouldn't have thought I'd be so keen on flowers. "So, you're big on honesty."

She lifted a shoulder. "I don't trust just anyone."

Her admission reminded me that I didn't either. A drop of condensation flowed over my fingers from the drink in my hand. I looked down at it and realized that during our conversation, I hadn't thought about the alcohol once. Picking up the drink, I examined it thoroughly, then placed it back on the napkin. "I'm not talking to you about the cage. I don't talk to anyone about that shit, and you're no exception."

"Is that what you think?" She leaned back, offended. "That I followed you here to try and get an interview?"

"You tell me. I've never seen you here before." I didn't mention that I'd never seen the inside of the joint myself.

"Me coming here has nothing to do with my job." The bartender walked back down to the end of the bar and asked what he could get her. "A pain-killer please."

Interesting choice.

"I'm Willow, since our introduction the other day wasn't exactly formal." She stuck her small manicured hand out for me to shake.

I had both my hands wrapped firmly around my drink, and believe it or not, it was hard to pull them away. "Conner." The bartender set

Willow's drink down, and I watched it sit there for a whole minute without her acknowledging it was there. "You going to drink that?"

"No."

"Then why order it?" I knew why I wasn't drinking mine. What was her reason?

"Liquor makes me gag. I'll have a glass of wine every now and then, but tonight is not about drinking for pleasure."

My eyebrow rose, but I remained silent, thinking about what she'd said.

"Do you come here often? Is this your place?" she asked.

I shook my head. "Never been here."

"Why now?" she asked. "Why tonight?"

"Why are you here?" I deflected.

"It's November twelfth."

I shifted my body to face her. "It is."

Her back stayed stiff and she stared at my drink. Her brow creased in concentration. She'd stopped talking altogether. I felt like an imposter watching her. Her head bowed slightly. Her small fingers traced a ring stain on the wooden bar. The sight of her being locked inside her own head should have made me more curious, but I respected that she seemed all too well with her own thoughts. I left her to her own, and brought my eyes back to my own problem.

We sat side by side, like the strangers we were, in complete silence.

"Conner?" She faced me after five minutes, giving me her full attention. Her legs spread so that my right knee sat between her legs, fitting perfectly.

Dragging my head in her direction, I looked at her.

"You up for a pinky swear?" She smirked. "I'm ready to do something big. I'm giving this ritual up, and I don't ever want to think about it again. No one knows about this part of my life. I'm ready to release it. It's held on to me for too long."

"You're willing to pinky swear with a dude you don't know?" It sounded ridiculous, but in that very moment, I knew I'd be willing to share with her too; completely trusting that she'd hold on to my secret, because she was so adamant that a pinky swear was the same thing as trust.

Her body leaned into mine, causing me to take a deep breath. "I trust you."

"You shouldn't."

"You're untrustworthy?"

I pursed my lips, thinking that was neither here nor there. Trust was a heavy thing, especially between strangers.

"I'm giving it to you anyway." Her chest rose and fell, completely calm. "I don't want it anymore. Once I tell you, I'm done with it. I'm living my life exactly the way I want to—without trepidation. I'll never fear it again. It won't touch me, scar me, or hold me back from this day forward."

"One question, before you spill your guts?" I asked.

"Shoot."

"Why a pain-killer? You ordered it like it's something you drink every day." I touched the rim of the glass. "This is no fruity drink."

"It sums up my addiction."

I felt exposed at her admission. The honesty in her blue eyes burst my armor at the seams. Like a piece of thread, holding together the last vestiges of my shield, it unraveled. "Why are you telling me this? We don't even know each other."

"I know a kindred spirit when I see one." She smiled to herself, but it wasn't a happy one. "I'm sort of addicted to pain. It has stalked me since I was a young girl."

Agony hit my gut; my senses on overdrive.

"When I was younger, and less intelligent, I opened my heart to someone unhealthy."

Silence surrounded us again. I didn't know how to respond to what she was saying.

"Long story short, I left myself exposed and hungry for something that I'm still not sure exists. I have no idea what I was chasing or why."

I nodded, letting her know I understood.

"I almost lost my life." She grunted a laugh and shook her head. "I literally threw everything away for a man. Or what I thought he stood for. And tonight? I'm giving it to you, Payne. I'm releasing it from my thoughts, from my heart, and I want you to scrounge up that intense, overpowering strength you have inside you and destroy it."

My eyes widened at her proposition. What was I going to do with it? I couldn't even kill my own demons. The blind faith she had in me boosted my courage as I thought about her words. I licked my lips, deliberating over my insecurities, and the instinct I had to protect her, even though I barely knew her.

I blew out a deep breath. I'd never confided in anyone before. Never expressed why I did the things I did. Palms clamming up, my nerves kicked into overdrive as I spoke. "I go out every November twelfth, no matter what is going on in my life, and I sit with a glass of whiskey. I note its color, the smell of it, and I stare it down, telling myself the whole fucking time that I won't drink it. I think about the damage it's done. I replay everything in my life that I fucked up. And the fact that this," I pointed to my drink, "has been the reason why, every single time."

She placed her hand on my thigh. At the comfort, I closed my eyes. She squeezed, and I tensed. She squeezed again, this time rubbing her thumb back and forth. When I glanced up at her, she had her eyes closed. I studied her face, dumbfounded. The action was intimate, and I ate it up like a damn baby.

I needed to hear her speak again. "You never answered my question." I nodded toward her drink. "Why the painkiller?"

She cracked her eyes open and stared at the bar. "To kill the pain."

"But you don't drink it."

"I don't need to." She pulled her hand away. "Why November twelfth?"

I shook my head slightly, signaling that I wasn't going to share that information. "I've got to head out." Scooting the stool back, I threw enough money on the bar for both our drinks and turned to go. "I train tomorrow."

"You forgot something," she said as I took two steps toward the door.

She slipped off the stool, her heels clinking against the wood floor. My gaze caught hers just before she made it in front of me. Blue eyes twinkling, she had a smirk spreading her full lips across her face. Standing at least a foot shorter than me, she held up her pinky.

I stared at it, amused at the thought of what she wanted me to do. Then she smiled and grabbed my pinky with her own. Fingers entwined, she brought them to her mouth and kissed her thumb. A dimple in her left cheek deepened, daring me to do the same. Her right eyebrow lifted, but I didn't cave.

When she saw that I wasn't going to play along, she flipped our hands around and kissed my thumb. Her eyes never left mine as her lips stayed cemented on my thumb, forcing me to engage in her stupid promise. As if we weren't adults, and couldn't just agree that our conversation would remain private.

Within seconds, her warm, pouty lips left my thumb and she released me, glancing back only once before walking away. I tilted my head to the ceiling and smiled. It would be a long time before the image of her ass in those pants would leave me.

The interaction left me feeling somewhere between relieved and captivated on my drive home. The funny thing was, I'd never felt better about leaving a drink untouched. I'd always, *always* regretted going out and engaging in an hour-long, self-loathing fest. But this time, I hadn't. This time, I left with a new temptation, and it didn't have shit to do with liquor.

Willow Stevens was elusive, yet friendly. Trusting, yet guarded. And even though she hadn't given me enough details to truly know her situation, I understood her need to look something in the eye and walk away from it, just to prove she could.

Pulling into my driveway, I knew I was screwed. I knew that she wore something on her lips to make them shine. I knew her hair was too wild to stay the way she initially fixed it because it kept moving out of place. I knew that she wore high-heels more than she wore flats, and she was comfortable in them. I knew she wore thongs or went commando because I looked at her ass enough to know there were no lines under the tight black pants she'd worn. My mouth watered just thinking about it.

Unlocking my front door, I stepped inside and leaned against it, letting my head fall back until it made contact. I frowned, knowing my growing infatuation for Willow Stevens was not a good thing. Not on a personal level, and not as a fighter, because Willow was a reporter, which meant she would eventually dig into my past.

I pushed off the door and walked straight to my bedroom, shedding my clothes on the way. I kicked off my jeans at the foot of my bed, and fell onto the mattress. Placing my arms behind my head, I regretted that we'd shared the moment together. But on the other hand, I wished it could have lasted all night.

I sighed and rolled over, pulling the sheet up to my waist. It wouldn't change anything—her knowing my truth. She'd never love someone like me. A man suffocating under a pile of guilt. A man trying to keep his head above water. Someone who was attempting to form a semblance of peace within himself, knowing that in all reality, he didn't deserve any of it. He was a killer. A true sucker for pain.

CHAPTER 6
WILLOW

"I DON'T GIVE a fuck what you write about. Just get it *out*." Andy's reddened face glistened with sweat. His eyes never paused on mine, he just talked to the room at large.

I watched my boss fumble around his office. He was out of sorts; not grasping that we still had three days to print. I hated what he'd become. It made me sad for him. "Andy," I said. When that didn't get his attention, I moved to stand. He still didn't acknowledge me, and I considered walking out and leaving him to his own demise, but I cared about the paper and my stories. I'd found my purpose in talking about other people's passions.

"I have to go," he said, looking off and to the right.

"What are you looking at?" I rounded his desk, and approached him.

"Can you, uh . . ." Sweat beaded on his upper lip. His eyes darted from side to side, as if he didn't know where to look.

"Andy." I clasped his elbow, turning him to face me. I waited, allowing him to see that I wasn't leaving until I said what I had to say. "I know what you're doing—what you're going through," I said, and softened my voice. "I want to help, if you're willing."

"What the fuck are you talking about?" He yanked his arm out of my hold. The burst of anger hadn't surprised me.

"You're all over the place. You don't even know what day it is."

Before I could even get another word out, he pushed me up against his desk without using his hands. He leaned so far into my face, that unless I wanted to kiss him, I had to lean back. His chest, mid-section, and thighs pressed hard into my front, making me shrink, even though I had enough adrenaline pumping through my body to probably throw him to the ground. I swallowed hard, considering my next words. His hot breath covered my face. I winced at the smell.

"You keep your nose out of my shit, and do your job. Unless you're offering what I think you are, stay the fuck out of my way." His nose touched mine, and my eyes nearly crossed looking directly into his.

"I'm not offering anything. I'm worried about you."

He pushed forward one last time, knocking me into a sitting position on his desk, his body pressing between my legs. "Just get the stories out, Willow." He eased back and walked out of his office.

I brought my shaky hands to my mouth, shocked that Andy had forced himself against me. My breaths came out in short pants, while I attempted to calm myself down. I knew going into it he'd be angry, and I also knew he could be an asshole when he wasn't high. But I hadn't expected to fear him.

I breathed out a sigh of relief that he was gone, and hung my head. I didn't want to work with him anymore. I had offered to help him, and he'd basically assaulted me—not to mention the sexual harassment he'd insinuated. That bastard was too far gone for me to handle. I'd start looking for a new job as soon as possible, but first and foremost, I needed to protect myself. Andy scared me. He made me feel like a victim, and I hated every second of it.

"Hey, girl. You just hanging out today, or looking for the next sucker to spill his guts?"

Steele had caught me off guard and I burst out laughing. He and I had become somewhat more than acquaintances—almost friendly. I liked him. I wasn't sure what he was going to think about why I was there, but I hoped he'd help me anyway.

"Actually, I was hoping to talk to you for a minute." I glanced around the gym, noticing only a few people lifting weights. No one was in the cage, so my uneasiness lightened a bit, knowing I probably wouldn't see any of the guys I'd already interviewed, or Conner.

His eyes narrowed with curiosity. He nodded and said, "Sure. Let's walk back to my office."

Steele stepped aside, allowing me to enter the back room first. I nodded my thanks as I passed by him. I still hadn't decided whether I was going to tell him everything or not. But I needed to be able to protect myself, and short of purchasing a gun, hand to hand was my only option. I took a seat hoping to calm my nerves.

"What's up?"

"I noticed you guys don't have very many women who train here."

"I don't discriminate, if that's what you're implying." He found a rubber band on his desk and stretched it out, before twisting it around his wrist.

I shook my head. "I'm sorry—that's not what I was implying." I took a deep breath, working up my courage. "Do you guys train women? Like self-defense type of stuff?"

"Why would you need self-defense?" He wasn't playing my game. I'd known before approaching him that he'd be inquisitive, but I hadn't planned on him coming straight out and asking me.

"It's good to know how to protect yourself. I'm not good with weapons, and I live alone."

He leaned forward, placing both his arms on the large desk calendar in front of him. I tried to not look away—it was the first sign of a lie—yet I couldn't help but focus on Payne's name in big block letters in one of the squares. I guess he had another fight coming up.

He rose from his chair and walked to the door. At first, I thought he was going to refer me to a gym down the street, but he didn't. He closed the door, then leaned his back against it, crossing his arms. He looked stern. His legs stood shoulder width apart as he considered his next words.

"What happened, Willow?"

"Nothing happened. I just—"

"All right. Here's the thing . . ."

I sat in silence as he approached me. He was careful, like he was trying to be sensitive, even though he was about to be brutally honest.

"If someone has touched you, that's something you need to share. I say that because, first and foremost, the asshole who touched you will be dealt with. After that happens, you need to go to the police and file a report."

"No, I swear, it was nothing like that. He just—he has problems. Bigger problems than any of us can help with, and well . . . things got a little out of control. He didn't touch me, but that particular situation made me think about how vulnerable I am. How I should be prepared, just in case."

"Who is it?" His clipped voice surprised me.

"I'd rather not say."

"Do I know him? Was it someone from the gym?"

"No. I promise." I placed my hands over my heart.

He studied me so long, I regretted even asking him now. Maybe I should have just asked Gage to show me a few moves. He would have never asked this many questions.

"I believe you," he finally said, blowing out a loud breath. "I don't have a specific class or anything like that, but I'd be willing to do something a couple of nights a week."

Relief rushed through me. "Thank you."

"I'll text you the dates. Bring Lena if you want."

"I appreciate this so much." I hugged him and he seemed surprised at the contact. "Seriously, thank you, Steele."

I walked out of the gym feeling determined. More people had shown up while I'd been in his office, but now that he'd agreed to help me, I wasn't so worried about looking out of place. I didn't even mind seeing Conner kickboxing in the corner. Gage whistled from the opposite side, making me smile. I winked at him and stole one last glance at Conner. He'd stopped his regimen all together. I continued walking, but glanced back at him one last time, right before I walked through the exit.

The next day, I called in sick to work. I wasn't ready to see Andy; having no way of knowing if he'd be high, or just coming down again. Either way, I wasn't in the mood. I'd just finished folding my laundry when a text came through.

Steele: You free today?

Me: Sure.

Steele: I'll be around the gym later. Come in, and we'll get started.

I finished my chores, anxiously awaiting my first lesson. I'd decided not to tell Lena, knowing she'd only worry, and until I found another job, it was best to keep my problems to myself.

My nerves still hadn't settled when I reached Trevor's gym.

"Hey! What's up, girl?" Gage held the door for me.

"Not much. Thought I'd get a workout in after a long day of working," I lied.

"Silly girl. You're supposed to workout first thing, that way you're not tired. If you're going to slack, you do that at your day job."

I laughed. Of course he felt like that. "Don't they teach the phenomenon of women in schools anymore? We can do it all, and do it well."

"I think I skipped that class." He hugged me. "Good luck!" He walked away with his gym bag over his shoulder. I faintly heard him whistling as the door closed.

I stood just inside, second-guessing myself the whole time. Now that I wasn't joking with someone, restlessness set in. The gym was quiet. Gage must have been the last one out. I turned back toward the door, thinking I could just text Steele that something came up, and never return again.

What in the hell am I doing here? Shaking my head, I forced myself to get over my self-doubt, deciding I wasn't a punk. I wasn't going to give up on defending myself. Even if I never used it, it was a good thing to know.

"Hey."

"Oh!" I jumped, more from my nervousness than being frightened. "You scared me." I'd been so inside my own head I hadn't noticed Conner walk in behind me.

"Sorry," he whispered as he slid past me. His shoulder bumped mine softly, almost as if he'd done it on purpose but tried to make it seem like an accident. It was cute, if that was what he was doing. I watched him walk with purpose to his corner, take off his shirt, pull his earbuds out, and tap his phone.

I wondered what kind of music he listened to. Probably metal.

Steele came from the back with a pile of towels. "You ready?" he asked, placing them in their bins.

"As I'll ever be." My anxiety skyrocketed with each word. "I wasn't expecting anyone else to be in the gym," I said softly, nodding toward Conner.

"We'll start slow." He glanced at Conner, then back at me. "Lena didn't want to come?"

"Maybe next time."

He studied me, then looked over at Conner again, who was doing a steady repetition on the boxing bag. Steele silently gave me a chance to elaborate, but I didn't. Once he realized I wasn't going to, he started out by having me stretch.

"I'm not an instructor or anything, but I feel like the first step in self-defense is being prepared. Having a plan if someone were to attack, knowing your surroundings, paying attention to your gut, and always having an exit plan."

"Got it." I finished the stretch he was demonstrating, and stood to my full height.

"No matter what situation you find yourself in, always yell loudly and push back. This will allow someone to hear you in your time of distress, but more importantly, it will let the attacker know you are not an easy target." He pushed his arms out in front of him in demonstra-tion. "Do everything with a purpose. If you're at the point of putting your hands on someone, you can't be gentle about it."

He signaled for me to try to push him as he approached. I did, but I didn't do it with enough force. "Sorry."

"Don't be sorry. We're learning here. Do it again, but this time, try to actually push me down." I pushed again, this time doing as he'd instructed. He rocked back on his heels.

"Good." He walked around me in a circle. "Okay, so once you're in that position where you have to defend yourself, you should know where to target. You'll want to hit the sensitive areas, and need to be quick and efficient."

"Sir, yes, sir!" I yelled, and he narrowed his eyes.

I heard a faint chuckle from the corner of the gym, and looked over at Conner in disbelief. I'd never even seen him grin before. The sight of him laughing melted me on the spot.

Steele eyed Conner, then settled back on me. I could tell he wanted to laugh too, but he held his composure. "Eyes, nose, ears, neck, and groin. You won't have a lot of time, so you need to be sure the places you hit make an impact."

He demonstrated an eye gouge, a punch to the nose, some weird slap to the ears, and a kick to the groin. I mirrored his movements, slow at first. After twenty minutes of repetition, I felt like I was actually learning something. We stopped to hydrate, then got right back into the swing of things.

As I continued the tactics he was teaching, I became comfortable in the way I was taking to the movements. I could feel Conner's attention on me, which caused tingles to break out all over my body. But I remained focused. I wanted my time spent with Steele to be productive because I might need the moves sooner rather than later.

"If the attacker is in front of you, use your palm like this," he pushed his palm up in front of my face, "and strike as hard as you can in an upward motion." He spun me around and grabbed me from behind. "If he is behind you, use an elbow."

"Like this?" I used my elbow to strike near his face. He must not have blocked my blow, as I heard him grunt, then felt a loss of his heat from my back.

"Damn." He coughed.

"Oh my god. I'm sorry. I thought you were ready." I put my hand on his back, trying to ease the pain.

"It's fine. I thought you were going to go for the ribs."

"Dumbass," Conner said as he stilled the bag he'd been punching. "You told her to go for the face."

"You want to train her?" Steele scowled at Conner as he rose to his feet.

My breath sped, and my heart leapt in my chest, half hoping he would, yet praying he wouldn't.

"Nah, I'm bouncing. See you tomorrow." He packed his bag, slung a T-shirt over his shoulders, then turned to leave. "Later, Willow."

His abrupt exit left me wanting more. More of what exactly? I wasn't sure. I just knew I frowned when he left, and I didn't smile again, even after I was home for the night and watching reruns of my favorite sitcom.

CHAPTER 7
CONNER

"DID you see Gunny broke his back? That means you'll be going up against—"

"Why was Willow here the other night?" I asked Steele, coming to a halt in front of his desk.

He looked up, surprised at first, but then his eyes softened, and his dimples appeared in a shit-eating grin. I'd been found out, and fuck if I cared. "Why, Payne? Why on Earth would you be asking questions about Willow?"

"Stop being a dick. Why was she here?" I was losing patience with his stupid game.

"Easy there, buddy." He laughed.

I wanted to throttle him for laughing at me. He knew me well enough to know I wasn't one to mess around. If I was asking him a question, it was because I wanted the answer. I took a moment to compose myself. Exhaling, I asked again. "Why are you teaching her to defend herself?"

"I honestly don't know." He laid some paperwork to the side and leaned forward, gearing up for our conversation.

"Is she in danger?"

"Why don't you ask *her*?" a soft voice said from behind me.

I blinked and turned to find Willow standing in the doorway of

Steele's office. "Okay," I agreed. "Why are you taking self-defense classes?"

She looked behind her, making sure there was no one in the hallway, then shut the office door and strolled into the office like a breath of fresh air. I tried not to dive head first into her deep blue gaze, like a twelve-year-old boy cliff diving for the first time.

She made her way to stand directly in front of me, still a head shorter in her four-inch cherry red heels. "I wanted to learn a few tactics, in case I ever needed them."

"Why would you need them?" I asked, barely noticing that Steele had stood and rounded his desk.

She blew out a puff of air that caused her bangs to flutter. "My boss is going through some stuff. He's all over the place, and he snapped at me the other day."

I was not expecting her to say that. I thought maybe she had a stalker, or a neighbor who was peering too long when she mowed her lawn. "Quit."

"I can't." She crossed her arms.

"Why?" I realized I was probably being a little demanding, and got confirmation when she pursed her lips.

"I'm working on other arrangements, but for right now, it is what it is."

"Bullshit. You can't go to work every day with a fucker you're scared of. That's stupid. Why would you put yourself in that position?"

She took a step toward me, not scared in the least. It made me wonder for a split second if she truly needed the lessons in the first place.

"I don't know who you think you are, but I'm not stupid. In fact, I count myself as an intelligent woman, and for someone, *anyone*, to suggest differently—well, let's just say, you may be the very first person who benefits from my classes."

"I didn't say *you* were stupid." I rolled my eyes at her putting words in my mouth. "I said staying where you don't feel safe is stupid."

Seconds ticked on as she looked like she might explode. I waited her out. I wanted to hear her reply.

"I hate to interrupt whatever *this* is, but you guys are making me uncomfortable." Steele made his way between us, putting an arm on each of our shoulders. "And Steele doesn't want to be uncomfortable in his own office, capeesh?"

Willow burst into laughter, and my muscles relaxed. Everything faded into the background as I watched joy take over her face. A part of me realized how dangerous she could be; the rest of me felt like a teenager again.

"Payne? Don't you have something to say to Willow?" Steele tried to lead me. But I didn't want to follow. I wasn't apologizing to her; I'd done nothing wrong.

Crossing my arms, I grunted. "I don't."

Steele grimaced. "What he means is, he's sorry he upset you. He knows not what he does."

"He doesn't look sorry."

"I'm not. I stand by what I said."

Her posture shrank. The fire in her eyes extinguished. "I'm not stupid."

Seeing that look on her face made me want to get down on my knees and grovel—beg her to forgive me. But I didn't. I didn't know what I could say. I'd rather have had the fire, knowing she was pissed, than the dull look she had now.

"If that's what you got out of our conversation, I guess there's nothing left to say." I nodded in her direction and left the room.

The further I got away from the room, the heavier my chest became. Genuine regret swallowed me whole as I walked the length of the hallway to the front exit of the gym. I hated that I'd snuffed the light out of her eyes. I thought I'd seen every color of blue imaginable, but I hadn't. Wounded blue may have been the most heartbreaking thing I'd ever seen, and I knew, in that moment, I never wanted to see it again.

Weeks passed while I wallowed in self-doubt. My latest opponent had suffered an injury, which meant I had a break. At least I'd been able to lick my wounds in private for the most part. I'd only gone to the gym in the middle of the night so that I wouldn't see anyone. Steele understood. He could see that I was playing it cool with Willow, because I wasn't sure if I wanted to pursue a relationship with her. He asked about it once. I told him it was none of his business. He nodded and walked away. I hadn't missed the smile that spread across his face as he did though.

Which also made me realize I was being dumb about the whole thing.

I searched the parking garage for a spot large enough for my truck. There weren't many. I ended up on a level lower than Willow's office. I hadn't planned on stopping by her work, but with each day that passed, I found myself feeling worse about the way I'd left things with her.

I took the stairs up to her office, and met a perky blonde at reception. "Hey. Um, I'm here to see Willow Stevens."

"Is she expecting you?" The headset she wore confused me. She was speaking to me, but looked as if she was listening to whoever was speaking to her through the wireless speakers.

"Yes, ma'am," I lied. She looked busy. Maybe she'd just wave me through.

"Second door on your left." She smiled, then continued with the customer on the phone. "I understand ma'am, but if you haven't paid for your subscription in two months, you can't expect to get a paper."

I'd never been in a professional building before. The interior was new, skillfully designed by the looks of it, and smelled like peppermint. She had a nameplate to the left of the door. *Fancy.*

"Andy, please," Willow's muffled voice could be heard through the door. There was an odd, overly soothing tone to it. I didn't like it at all.

I slipped my hand in my pocket, wondering if I should just leave. But my curiosity won out and I glanced around to make sure no one was in the hallway.

"I don't—"

"Stop jerking me around, Willow," a male voice interrupted.

My whole body tensed as the sound of bodies moving and papers scattering filled the silence. The hand in my pocket balled into a fist.

"Listen to me. I know you're using. I see it. Everybody sees it." Her voice lowered. My curiosity surged. I opened the door, not caring that I was interrupting.

"You don't know shit." Andy stood, and walked out, pushing past me in the doorway. My insides lurched at the thought of stopping him. I almost blocked his path, but Willow remained silent, so I let him pass.

"What's going on?" I asked, keeping my distance.

"Nothing."

"Seriously, *that's* what you're going with?" I stared her down, not allowing any wiggle room for her to deceive me.

She huffed out a breath, and crossed her arms. "It's a long story."

"I got time." I shrugged.

"And this is why you just happened to stop by my office out of the blue? To listen to my story?" she pressed.

"Nah, I came here to apologize for being a prick the other day."

She stared at me and chewed the inside of her cheek, before a grin spread across her face. "You interested in some coffee?"

"Sure," I lied. *Not coffee, just you.*

I followed at a snail's pace behind Willow as she drove the whole way to her house under the speed limit. I had offered to drive us from her office, but she'd declined. I couldn't be sure why, but I was fairly certain her rejection hadn't been because she didn't want to spend time with me—considering she'd invited me to her home.

Pulling into her drive, I took a moment in the cab of my truck to push my worries back. The last thing I wanted to convey to her was fear. Not after she'd just been so strong in dealing with a junkie. I tucked my keys into my back pocket and met her in the garage.

"Just let me change right quick. I'll start the coffee first," she said as she unlocked the door, and clicked the garage opener, causing daylight to be closed off as the large door shut.

I took a seat on the sofa in her living room, while different scenarios ran through my mind. The longer she took to change clothes, the crazier my ideas got. I wanted to know who the guy was, and why she had problems with him. Had they dated in the past? Why would he argue like that with an employee? What kind of dope was he on?

Willow shuffled into the living room, wearing black yoga pants, an oversized sweatshirt, and light purple house shoes. She looked beautiful. Her hair was twisted up into a messy looking bun, pieces of it falling around her face. I inhaled deep as she took a seat next to me on the sofa.

Relaxed, I glanced around for the first time. Her house was eclectic. Her furniture sat catty-corner in the small living room, but the bursts of color from the picture frames and throw pillows were comforting somehow. There were small details all over her home, telling me she'd spent time on decorating the space. She was good at it too.

She tucked a teal-colored pillow under both arms, while pulling both legs underneath her to get more comfortable.

"What's he on?" I asked.

"I'm not sure." She shrugged. "I think meth. Maybe coke."

"He didn't hurt you, did he?"

"No. It's been mostly verbal stuff," she said.

I leaned forward and placed my elbows on my knees, knowing she might not like what I was about to suggest. "You need to type up a resignation letter."

"I'm not quitting yet."

"Willow . . ." I wasn't sure what to say. I closed my mouth, then opened it again, and still, nothing came out. I wrestled with my thoughts as we stared at each other in silence. "You need to go to the police. That dude is a fucking psycho."

She studied me cautiously. I'd never been one to shy away from a challenge, but as I sat there, next to the woman I'd considered letting get to know the real me, I was petrified. I'd been able to handle whatever life had thrown at me, in whatever form, but being rejected by her wasn't something I wanted to feel. It wasn't that I thought she'd judge me, so much as she wouldn't want to take a chance on me.

"I'll think about it," she finally replied. Then she added, "This isn't the first time I've dealt with a junkie, you know."

I swallowed, hating hearing her words. She was too pure. Too beautiful and smart to have been subjected to something so ugly. "Who?"

"When I was younger, I may have been a little rebellious." She looked up at me and continued. "My first love—or what I thought was love—was reckless and wayward. He was selfish, and never thought beyond where the next party was."

I nodded, bashing myself on the inside, because honestly, it sounded like she was describing me. And I didn't want to be anything like the person who'd hurt her.

"I guess, I just didn't really know who I was, or who I wanted to be at the time, so every time he'd tell me how special I was, or how much he loved me, I would just chalk his addiction up to us being young. At first, anyhow. Looking back on it, he was abusive. Not physically, but emotionally. It got to a point where I didn't care about myself."

She hugged her middle and shivered, like she was dead-center in the middle of a horrible memory. "For the longest time, I tried to help him. But over time, I just gave up. I gave up on him. I gave up on me. I just sort of threw my hands in the air. My memories from that time in my life feel as if I'd been buried alive. Almost suffocating."

I shook my head, knowing all too well what she was saying. Knowing how, even though no one ever wanted to think about giving up, sometimes there didn't seem to be much to live for.

"Long story short; I caught him cheating. Walked in right in the middle of it and swallowed the first pile of pills I found."

My gut clenched. I couldn't picture her, this beautiful creature sitting in front of me, being so low.

She wiped a lone tear away from the corner of her eye. "Your silence is deafening."

"I hate that you did that. I hate that a man treated you like that. And I really fucking hate that I can relate to it in any way."

"You can?" she asked.

I nodded. "I can. Not with the dude part though." She giggled. "But being so low. Not knowing what to do. Partying, like life doesn't matter." I pushed my fingers through my hair.

"I just wanted you to know. I'm not sure what's going on here," she pointed from her chest to mine, "but I figured being honest was the way to go."

Honesty.

It might have been just one word, but the weight of it could have cracked the foundation we seemed to be building. I glanced up at her, knowing I needed to tell her, but still not wanting to.

"Just say it, Conner. You won't scare me away, I promise."

"I'm an alcoholic."

Her eyes narrowed for a split second. Our gazes never wavered. Neither of us blinked, waiting to see what the other was going to do. I was waiting for her to kick me out. She was waiting on me to elaborate. She won.

"I started drinking as a teen. Mostly for fun, other times it was out of sheer boredom. Then, there was like, years that went by, you know?" I rubbed my hands together, more from nerves than anything else. "I just lost control of it. I gave in to it a little bit each day, and it snowballed."

"You're not drunk now." She nudged my leg. "That means you've obviously found courage from somewhere, and changed your life. Look at what you're doing now with fighting."

Her attempt at encouragement fell on deaf ears. There hadn't been a moment of clarity for me. I got locked up and dried out over a nine-year sentence. "I wish I could tell you it happened that way."

"How did it happen?"

"You first." I knew I had to tell her. I knew there was something between us; something that could last for a long time. And lying to her, or trying to hide who I really was, would delay the inevitable.

She licked her lips, picked at her nails, and blew her bangs out of her face, before leaning back. I wasn't exactly sure she was going to share her truth, until she murmured, "I almost died. I overdosed that night. The night I took all those pills." Her eyes shown brighter. "You know that feeling you get when you realize everything has a purpose? Like when it finally dawns on you that you're here for a reason? And you feel like you've wasted so much time on people who don't matter."

She scooted closer to me, drawing her knees underneath her ass to sit on her legs. "I sort of had that realization when I woke up in the hospital. I knew I had to change; that I was *worth* the change."

I grabbed her hand without a second thought. We both stared down at our intertwined hands, silently. It was as if there was a gravitational pull, tugging me closer to her as I listened to her recount the worse day of her life. There was an obscurity inside her part of me wanted to hang on to for dear life. The other part of me wanted to reveal the absolute darkest part of my soul to steer her away.

"I've made so many mistakes, Willow. So damn many. And I can attribute alcohol to nearly all of them. I've struggled. I've altered other people's lives because of my choices. But, right now, sitting here with you, wanting nothing more than to kiss your lips . . ." I lifted my free hand and grazed her plump bottom lip with my thumb. "I feel like none of that matters."

She leaned in, giving me the go ahead. I brought her mouth to mine, brushing my lips gently across hers. Her hair grazed my jaw, only making me more crazed. I turned my head, so I could deepen the kiss. Stealing every breath I could, I placed both hands under her arms and moved her until she was straddling my lap, never once breaking our kiss.

My mind was blank. Negativity ceased to exist when I had Willow in my arms. Insecurity fell to the wayside; my only concern involved being in the moment with her.

My hands wanted to roam. My pelvis wanted to push into her heat to create friction.

The doorbell rang, and she ran her tongue along mine one more time before pulling back.

I groaned in frustration. "Expecting someone?"

Willow shook her head and shrugged, making her way to the door. When she opened it, there was a mailman standing there, holding a box. The fucking mailman interrupted me from sucking on her lips. What in the hell could have been so important that he couldn't have just left the package at the door?

I closed my eyes and breathed in deep, attempting to calm my body, while Willow stood at the door, carrying on a full-blown conversation with her mailman about the new neighbor. She probably seemed normal to him, but I knew she was conversing with him sidetracked— and flushed cheeks because of our previous make-out session. Her sweatshirt was wrinkled because we'd just been body to body on her couch. I continued to watch them in silence—a sly grin on my face from the brief memory. In fact, I was still grinning when she closed the door and sat the package in an arm chair.

She crossed the living room floor, with a seductive upturn to her lips.

It was at that very moment, dread filled my gut. I'd never *not* wanted to talk to someone so bad in all my life, but I knew, if I had any chance with Willow Stevens, it was now or never. I couldn't let things go any further until I spilled the beans.

Just before she reclaimed her spot on my lap, I stood and paced the length of the living room like a dog in a cage. I counted to fifty before I spoke. "I have something else to tell you."

CHAPTER 8
WILLOW

"TELL ME." I could tell whatever he was about to admit was hard for him. I typically liked quiet people. I'd always been drawn to them. I loved that I never knew where they stood, or what they were thinking. They could've been a hundred miles away or fantasizing about a cupcake for all I knew. But now that I was witnessing the shadows behind Conner's eyes, the anxiousness and vulnerability in them, I silently wondered what the appeal ever was.

He wiped his palms on his jeans and pulled his bottom lip between his teeth, setting off alarm bells in my mind.

"Conner?" I spoke gently, almost as if I were talking to a child.

He stopped and looked at me for the first time since he'd started pacing. "Yeah?"

I patted the seat cushion. "Come sit beside me." I wanted to hold his hand, so he wouldn't feel so alone.

He sat down, awkwardly putting off a restless energy. I brought our hands together, squeezing once for comfort. He took in our clasped hands, then smiled sadly to himself.

"I used to be in real estate," he said, his voice thick with memory. "Had a decent life. Made decent money." He shrugged and sighed. "This is fucking hard."

I thought he was going to pull away from me. The storm brewing in his eyes frightened me. He was struggling, and I wasn't used to seeing him like that. His hands trembled in mine. His right leg bounced with nerves, and I worried he would back out. Or that what he was going to tell me would be unforgivable.

He blew out a deep breath and looked me straight in the eyes. "I trust you. And I'm not sure why. I've never felt the need to tell someone this."

Seeing the look in his eyes, the way his knee pressed tightly against mine, and the complete crack in his outer appearance, hit me like a ton of bricks. It was as if my body had forgotten the simple task of breathing. Tightness filled my chest, causing me to exhale slowly. I made no fast movements because I was afraid he might spook and not finish.

"Nine years ago, I drove drunk, had a wreck, and killed the driver of the other vehicle."

My brain buzzed, so many thoughts circling; dizziness shook me, making me feel lightheaded. Someone died. Conner was no killer. He couldn't have been responsible for taking an innocent life. Could he? But he just told me he was.

Sympathy flooded every cell in my body and I exhaled a breath I hadn't realized I'd been holding. I couldn't believe he'd had to live with something so heavy. No wonder he was wounded. Carrying that burden seemed almost unreal. I'd made mistakes. Many of them. But all the bodily pain I'd ever caused had been to myself. I'd never hurt anyone else. Not physically anyway. My heart broke for him.

"I'm so sorry," I said, and moved our clasped hands onto his thigh as I leaned closer to him. "I'm sorry that happened."

"You have no idea."

I pulled him closer. I might have needed the intimacy as much as him, but either way, I had to console him. I wrapped my arms around his shoulders and clutched him so tight, it seemed as if I were the stronger one. He leaned into me and I held him.

After a while, I pulled away, but still kept contact. I had questions. Before I could ask them, he spoke again.

"I went to prison. I'm a convicted felon."

I fought to keep my composure, but my eyes widened. There was such vulnerability in his voice; something so sincere, I couldn't look away. I found myself wanting to fix all his hurts because I could see just how deep they were burrowed into the depths of his soul. Not only had Conner ended someone else's life, he'd lost his own for a while too.

"I get if this is too much, I just—well," he said and pulled away. "I thought if we were going to hang out, you should know."

Cool air hit my legs as he created space between us. I pressed my hand on his thigh, rooting him in his spot. "I appreciate you telling me." I chewed on the inside of my cheek, wishing I had more to say. My gaze dropped to his large, tanned hands that were constantly ringing each other. Swallowing, I added, "Thank you for today. I don't know what would have happened if you'd not shown up."

"It was nothing." He shrugged. "I'm just glad you're okay."

The silence grew, taking on a life of its own. I didn't know what to say. How could I ever heal that part of him? It had taken me years to forgive myself for not loving myself enough to care what happened to me. Years.

I couldn't imagine taking the responsibility of ending someone else's life, and putting that in a box in my brain, where I could live with it and accept it. A place where I could still be okay—

have peace in my life. I ached for him bone deep, knowing all the support in the world wouldn't fix the hurt he carried around with him every day. I wanted to tell him that everything would be okay, and that we'd figure it out, but I couldn't promise that to be true.

"I'm going to go," he announced as he stood. "Give you some time to digest everything. It's cool either way, really." Tucking his hands into the pockets of his jeans, he appeared less confident than I'd ever seen him. His gaze met mine head on. "I'd appreciate if we could keep what I told you just between us."

"Conner, I'd never . . ." I reached out to touch his arm, but pressed my hand to my stomach instead. "You can trust me."

Pain flickered in his eyes as they focused on my middle. His shoulders fell forward as he nodded, then he walked toward the front door, leaving me wanting to reach for him.

"Wait," I called.

Stretching my pinky out to him, Conner stared out my outstretched hand. He didn't smile, but the indention between his brows eased, becoming less prominent. He took hold of my pinky, and pressed his thumb to his lips. "I'll see you around, Willow. I'm sorry about—well, about everything. If you need anything, you know where to find me."

Before I could thank him again, he walked out.

I stood in turmoil at the large bay window, and watched him drive away. Hollowness hit the pit of my stomach. It hurt. I felt as if I'd just lost something I never quite had.

After failed attempts at filling the weird void somehow left by not confessing some kind of commitment to Conner, I figured focusing on myself would be less stressful. Instead of affording Andy the respect of a resignation letter, I simply chose not to return to work. I should have gone to the police. Quitting a lower-middle income should have been the least of my worries. Alas, money made the world go round.

"Know anybody hiring?" I asked the second Lena picked up my call.

"Why?"

I sighed. "I quit my job."

"What?"

"Andy's a dick. He tried to come onto me, and I think he's on something. He's a freaking mess."

"Gross. He didn't touch you, did he?"

I was glad we were on the phone. If we had been together, she would have picked up on my lies. "No. He was aggressive though. He cornered me in the office, and Conner walked in at the end of it. It was intense."

She gasped. "Wait. Conner? What did he say?"

"Conner was—concerned." I grimaced at the memory. "But thankfully, Andy left before things got out of hand."

"And why was Conner at your office? You little minx! Are you guys hooking up?"

"No. Well, I think we possibly could have, had he not walked in on me and Andy arguing, but—it's complicated."

She laughed. "What's complicated? He's hot, Will. Go for it."

If only it were about his looks. That part was definitely not complicated.

"I don't know. We're talking though." It wasn't exactly a lie.

"I've got a meeting in five. I'll come over after work, and I'm bringing wine."

I loved my friend for the thought, but I had a feeling it wasn't going to touch the troubles I had going on at the moment.

Two hours later, my eyes were crossing. I'd searched every classified ad within a thirty-mile radius. After ten emails and two phone calls, it seemed I had three possibilities. Working in a bar wasn't my first pick, but I'd do what I had to do until I could find something else. Next was a local newspaper—my old rival—but I'd not burned any bridges with their editor, so I was hoping my chances were good. The last was a women's magazine, which included working from home. Freelancing, basically. I would have rather talked to someone personally, but they were only taking applications online.

I'd fought the urge to drive down to the gym all day. Finding that even with all the confusion and uncertainty of where Conner and I left things, all I wanted to do was see him. I wanted to comfort him, and make up for every sad thought he'd had since the last time I saw him.

My urge won out.

The lights were still on, but Steele's Jeep was the only one in the parking lot. I glanced around, taking in my surroundings before I walked to the door. It was locked, so I knocked a few times, hoping he could hear me. In my edginess, I rocked back and forth on my heels, with my arms crossed tightly over my chest. It was dark, and cooler than I'd expected. My long-sleeved T-shirt did little to keep the chill from my body.

His expression as he unlocked the door told me he wasn't exactly happy to see me. Either that, or he was surprised. Once I made my way inside, there was no doubt it was the former.

"What's up?" he asked.

"I want to talk to you, if you have a minute."

"Look. I'm not really cool with getting involved in Conner's shit. I like you, Willow. And I know he likes you, but if you have questions, you need to ask him."

Obviously, I wasn't hiding my emotions very well. "I get that." The confidence I'd just had moments before dwindled at his words. "I'm not looking for his life story. Well, not from you, I guess. I'm just confused. I need someone who is not me, for reasons I won't go into right now, to reassure me that he's solid. Deep down, I know he is, but what he told me about his past shocked me."

"I'm not sure what you want me to say. I don't know what he shared with you, and it's none of my business. But I will tell you that Payne is one of the best dudes I've ever met. We're tight."

"I know this is weird, and probably a little immature on my part." I tucked a piece of my hair behind my ear. "I like him. I do. But my track record with bad boys is longer than I care to admit. I don't want to put myself in a situation where I'm vulnerable to anything toxic. And for the life of me, I don't think he is, but my feelings for him already scare me. After all the years I've invested in myself, making myself a stronger person, I just want to make sure what I'm feeling for him isn't blinding me."

Steele shook his head, as if trying to convince me I was wrong about his friend. He rounded the tall counter in the lobby and took a seat on the stool, settling in for our conversation. He was more relaxed now, but hadn't let his guard down. His hands were clasped on top of the counter, as if he were speaking to a client instead of a friend. "He's got issues, but we all do. If you're suggesting he's toxic, I'd have to disagree."

"Oh God, no. That's not what I was saying. I just—I care about him. And I want to make sure that if he and I were to make a go at it, it would be a positive thing for both of us." I didn't want him to misunderstand what my concerns were. I only wanted to talk to someone who knew Conner better than anyone. And since I wasn't ready to speak to Conner just yet, I figured voicing my uncertainties to his best friend would garner me an honest opinion.

"Look, we all have a past. All of us." He pointed to himself, letting me know he wasn't excluded. "If we walked around judging everyone on mistakes they'd made two, five, or even ten years ago, none of us would have friends."

Talk about putting me in my place.

His words cut deep; flaying me open, he showed me what a hypocrite I was being. The truth was, I had secrets I was harboring too.

And maybe Conner wouldn't be able to deal with my baggage. I realized I'd come here looking for something that didn't exist. No one could validate my feelings. No one could take responsibility for my insecurities. No one could forgive me for my own choices. That was an inside job.

"You're right. I'm just scared, I guess. As you said, we've all got skeletons. I have to talk to him; tell him how I feel." I smiled, thinking about the new revelation.

"You do that, but keep in mind that he has a fight in less than a week. He doesn't need to be worn out." He winked. Now *that* was the Steele I knew. "He's got his eye on the prize, and I need him focused. His chances with the AFL are good."

"Shut up."

His dimples appeared when I picked up on his perverse comment. And with that, Steele's demeanor relaxed. He'd just been looking out for his friend, and I couldn't blame him.

I hugged him and whispered in his ear. "I'm going to take care of him."

He squeezed me tight, lifting me in the air. Just like that, the weight of our conversation had evaporated, and returned to the light-hearted friendship we'd been steadily building.

CHAPTER 9
CONNER

"I'M NOT that familiar with Upton's ground work," Steele said. "But I've seen a few videos, and he leans right a ton. He's weak on the left side, so take advantage of that."

"Got it," I said.

I'd been training nonstop for the past week. I was man enough to admit to myself that most of it had been to keep my mind off Willow. I hadn't seen her once, nor had I heard from her. Not that she had my number, but there were other ways to get a hold of me. She'd not been to the gym, and that pissed me off more than anything because she needed to keep up with her lessons. I didn't want to be the reason she wasn't committed to learning how to protect herself.

I hadn't slept a full five hours in six days. My body was heavy, my head clouded, and my breathing labored. I wasn't anywhere near ready to fight. But no one cared about that; the show must go on. And so, I entered the cage, for the first time in all my time training, defeated before I even threw the first punch. My mind was tormented with doubt. I peered back at Steele, feeling like I was letting him down somehow.

I didn't even remember the referee signaling. I took so many punches, I stopped counting at ten. I rolled a couple of times, locking and loading on my opponent, but was unable to get a good grip on an ankle lock. I knew the moment he rolled me over, I was done.

Rolling forward, I escaped his attempt at a choke hold. Standing up, dizziness overtook me, and I thought I was going to faint. I tried twice to dodge his fist and failed. My feet were planted flat on the ground, and it felt like I had cinder blocks attached to them. I wasn't strong enough to pick one foot up and place it in front of the other. My vision blurred, lightness turning to darkness as I tried to make it to my corner. I fell, just short of reaching the cage, and landed on the ground like a ton of bricks. Knocked out.

I came to with Steele at my head, slapping my cheeks. I looked around the cage, unsure of the moments prior. The last thing I remembered was stumbling around.

"Morning sunshine." His expression was tense, even though his voice sounded light-hearted. "You good?"

"Yeah." I tried to sit up. Extreme nausea swirled in my gut causing me to fall back.

"Hold tight." His voice trailed off.

Coming to, I winced, barely able to make out the locker room. I'd passed out again. Somehow, I ended up on the medic table. Pushing myself up, I leaned on my elbow in an attempt to sit up. Pain shot through my chest, causing me to re-think my next move. Breathing even hurt. I reached for my ribs, but a warm hand touched my side.

"Hey. You're okay."

I shook my head, thinking I was hallucinating. Willow's voice was soft as a lullaby. I listened as she told me over and over how to take slow and steady breaths. Just like a song, I breathed to the rhythm of her voice.

After a couple of hours, the house doctor cleared me to go home. I felt fine at that point, other than my injuries, but Steele and Willow both discussed taking care of me as if I were a child. I shut up and listened, more so because my head pounded steady enough to make me feel like throwing up, and also because I didn't have anything to say. I tried not to think about it too much, given the shape I was in, but I'd just lost a fight. Losing wasn't a feeling I was familiar with. Not in the cage anyway.

The biggest problem with the loss was that I had beaten myself. I'd given my opponent the win, and I didn't understand why. Out of all the shit I'd been through in my life, I'd never given up. Until now. I'd thrown in the towel before the bout had even begun. In light of my revelation, I wanted to go home. I wanted to be alone; to lick my wounds in private like a normal loser. To top off the loss, I needed to wrap my head around the fact I was willing to lie flat on my fucking back for a girl. One who'd all but rejected me.

"I'll take good care of him." Willow was all business, her hand rubbing my arm. "I will call you if we need anything."

"Watch him," Steele told her. "He'll be okay, just try to keep him up for a while."

"I promise." Willow walked out of the locker room.

"You good?" Steele asked me, walking around the table.

"Yeah, man." I sat up, fighting the constant nausea. "I will be."

"Payne, I—"

"Don't." I could see the questions behind his eyes. I could hear the sincerity in his voice.

"What happened?" he asked anyway.

"I don't want to talk about it."

Of all the fucked-up shit I'd done in my life, I could only think of one other time I'd been so ashamed of myself.

He nodded in understanding, but I knew he wasn't going to let it go. It wasn't in his nature. "We'll talk later."

Willow re-entered the room like a tornado. Moving quickly to my locker, she picked up both my bags, grabbed my keys and phone, and moved toward me looking like a high school football manager. I wondered how she was able to carry all my shit, knowing everything probably weighed more than she did.

"I pulled the car up to the back door," she said. "Get him there, and I can do the rest."

"What about when you get home?" he asked.

"I got this, Steele," she snapped.

Had I been in my right mind, I would have laughed at his face. He was genuinely concerned, although he knew I'd be okay. I hadn't noticed before, but looking at her now, Willow was pissed. Her brow creased severely, and her shoulders were stiff walking ahead of us. I leaned on Steele for support as we followed her to her car at a much slower pace. Willow stuffed my belongings into the back seat, then opened the passenger side door. She waited, what appeared to be impatiently, as Steele and I made it to her car.

Once I had fallen into the seat, she leaned over me, buckling my seatbelt. Had I any energy, I would have brought her into me. I would have smelled her, and touched her skin, and reveled in the sensation while doing it. But there would be none of that tonight.

After making sure I was settled, she slid out the passenger side door, and walked back to the driver's side, without so much as a smile in my direction. I could hear her talking to Steele outside the vehicle. I couldn't hear what they were saying though, and I didn't much care. My head was pounding.

"Can you turn the air on?" I asked as we made our way onto the highway. Sweat beads formed at my hairline. I took a deep breath and winced at the pain in my side.

"Sure. Whatever you need, right?" The sarcasm was thick.

At her curtness, I opened one eye, while squinting with the other. I hadn't even looked at her since we'd started on our path to either my house or hers, I wasn't sure. I closed the eye that was open, gingerly leaning back in the seat, and dozed off.

"Come on, dummy! I can't carry you *and* all your shit."

I awoke to her voice, and her tugging on my arm. It was an ill attempt, as I was still buckled into the seatbelt. I batted her hand away and felt around for the buckle. Once I was free, I pushed myself up, feeling unbalanced. I walked, with her help, up to my front door.

She fumbled with the keys, trying the wrong one before she was able to unlock the door. I held a chuckle in at the fact I only had two keys on the ring. The other was for my truck. She was out of sorts and frantic in her movements, even though everything around me seemed to stand still.

"Get on the couch, and I'll put your things away."

"Thanks." It wasn't like she heard me, as she'd already started down the hallway.

I stumbled over and fell into the cushions. I wished I had a pillow, but there was no way in hell I was asking her for anything. Not with the mood she was in.

"Wake up, Conner. Conner? Steele said to keep you awake."

"I'm awake," I lied.

"No, you're not."

I leaned up, adjusting myself in a halfway seated position, but couldn't find any comfort. I slid back into the corner of the couch, trying to clear my head enough to prepare for what she was about to dish out. "What's your problem?"

"My problem?" She walked out of the room, only to return seconds later. I noticed she looked awfully comfortable in my small home, considering she'd never been there before. She punched the pillow from my bed, making me flinch each time, and then stuffed it behind my head.

"Look, I'm fine. You don't have to stay." I didn't want her to feel obligated.

"Shut up." Her eyes blazed with anger.

The pain had started to subside, not from healing, but because I was focused on her. I grabbed her wrist with more grip than intended, and pulled her onto the couch next to me. "What's the deal? Why are you being like this?"

"I'm pissed."

"Why? Not that I would remember at the moment, but I don't recall doing anything to you." The vein in my temple thumped in time with my heartbeat.

"Seriously? You didn't do anything to me? God, you're dense."

I shook my head, squinting in agony as the throbbing intensified. "I'm not following."

"Out of all the fights I've been to, I have never—*ever*—seen anything like that. Do you have any idea how scared I was? Do you know what you put me through watching that shit show?" Tears formed in her eyes and it seemed like every time they were ready to fall, her eyelids would suck them back in.

My shoulders fell at her admission. "Sometimes, I feel like I hate you," I whispered. Fighting off the pain, I pulled her into my arms.

I'd wanted to say love. Sometimes, I felt like I loved her, and it was complete and total crap. I'd barely spent any time with her, but at the same time, I didn't need to. Everything about her made me gravitate toward her. Her hair, her body, her smile, her smell, the way she called me a dummy when she was pissed—all of it. But most of all, I knew I could trust her. There was no substitute for that.

Her body relaxed as she snuggled into me. I wasn't sure she'd gotten my joke until she said, "I hate you too, especially when I see you hurt. That makes me despise you." She hugged me tight, bringing my body flush with hers.

It was fucked up, but in a weird way, almost a defense-mechanism-way, we were both admitting our feelings for each other. I'd just told her I loved her in my own way and she'd done the same. Anyone who could evoke the feelings I felt with her had my heart, whether they wanted it or not. Even if it was shredded and harder than stone. Another surprise, she didn't seem to mind.

After allowing the heavy emotions that were tied to my fight to wear off, we stayed up all night talking about our childhoods, debating whose was worse. I won that sad competition. Willow told me about her mom, and how she couldn't wait for me to meet her. I smiled at all the right moments, but didn't disclose much about my own mother. I confided to Willow that my mom had all but disowned me, and left it at that. I didn't feel the need to put that much negativity out in the open, being that it was basically our first night together.

I learned that Willow and Lena had become friends quickly, and that she counted her as one of her closest confidantes. She was Willow's Steele. I told her the story of how Steele and I met, and how it took me a couple of times at the gym before I actually talked to him. She was curious about how I came to fight, so I told her. In the beginning, it was more due to Steele badgering me, and also a way to make money. Not so much after tonight, but before then, I had begun to see it as a career opportunity. Steele was doing it, why not me? Well, tonight was one of the reasons I was not ready. Quitters didn't deserve a chance at going pro.

Clarity formed somewhere between the top half of my body softening, and the bottom half ready to burst through my clothes like the Hulk. God, she felt good; cuddled so close to me, I could smell her shampoo and feel every contour of her body. I ran my hands over her, as I memorized every curve, every soft patch of skin, and the way her hour-glass figure was dramatized when she was turned onto her side.

I lifted her shirt, calculating every move. I even went as far as having her nod for confirmation. Too much too quick could compromise how far we'd come in such a short amount of time, and the last thing I wanted to do was screw up the natural flow of things. I finally knew what it meant to love someone. A woman who I never wanted to give up. The one I needed to touch. The woman I didn't mind sharing the intricate parts of me with. Going back to my childhood hadn't been as bad as I thought it to be. At least, not with her.

My palm slid firmly from her ribcage into the dip of her waist, then up and over her smooth hips. God, I wanted to put my mouth on her. Pain was the last thing on my mind. My muscles, as tight as they were, felt like putty. My adrenaline spiked as she made a small, contented sigh, and placed her head under my chin. Her eyelashes tickled my skin when they fluttered closed.

She stayed silent, letting me explore her. Goose bumps sprinkled across her bare skin. My palm searched her softness, as if my thirst would be quenched by her preciousness. I had a moment where I wanted to look in her eyes, so I could pinpoint every twinkle, all the times they widened with each move I made, but I wouldn't interrupt our rhythm.

Like a blind man going through life, I paced my traces in time with the beat of my heart. Every thump, my fingertips inched upward, until I was unbuttoning her blouse and cradling her forward, so I could undress her.

She kept her eyes closed as I did away with her blouse, not even noticing its color. Her bra though—that was black. My index finger fondled the lace just beneath the wire holding her perfect breast in place. My thoughts of seeing her eyes fell by the wayside as I took in her bare skin. Leaning over her, I pulled her close, causing her back to fall onto the cushions as I took my place on top of her.

I couldn't recall another time I'd ever felt so turned on. Sure, I'd had multiple partners along the way—some of them even more experienced than I'd been—but I had never witnessed more beauty in one person. The arch of her back. The silkiness of her skin. Her long hair splayed out behind her. She was perfection. She was mine.

Rubbing the spot I'd picked out moments before, I pressed my lips against hers. I'd imagined the feel of it a million different ways, but peaceful hadn't been one of them. Kissing her again made me happy. Not satisfied. Not sated. Not even content. I smiled without control, each time my tongue slipped inside her mouth.

Willow's soft sighs and small movements engulfed my body like music. Just like the beat of a killer song, she had my body gyrating in time with her breaths. We were in perfect sync as I slid the cups of her bra up and took the tip of her rose-colored nipple into my mouth. I never wanted to let go.

Her fingers pushed through my hair, tugging gently until she reached the ends. My headache was gone. There was not one sign of discomfort from my fight earlier. All I could feel was her. The way I felt with her in my arms. Our quick, rapid breaths matched, our chests close enough to move together. She was as worked up as I was, and I reveled in the fact that I had a hand in her feeling that way. As my lips worked every square inch of her breast, my fingertips barely grazed her thighs. She kicked her shoes off and dug her heels into my ass.

Closer.

Closer.

Closer.

She willed me to be closer to her, and I wanted to be. I ground my arousal into her center as hard as I could. I needed her to remember me. To leave a mark on her soul. I wanted her to experience a different kind of pain. Not insecurities about where I'd been, or where we would go. Not thinking about being cornered by her sleazy boss. Not hurt because she'd just witnessed her man lay down and lose without ever trying. No. I wanted the aching to go so far beyond hurting, that it actually felt good.

My body moved against hers in a cadence that hauled moans from the back of her throat. And when I took her to the next level, without ever losing our clothes, the amount of pride I had took me so high, I was afraid to come down.

"Conner." Her hands slid from the back of my head to my chin, where she absently fondled the hair there.

I wondered if she regretted letting me touch her. It hadn't been something I'd ever concerned myself with before. Rejection happened, then you moved on to the next woman. That had been a given. But with Willow, I didn't want to move on.

I hated myself in that moment. There was something parallel with her and alcoholism. The lure felt similar to the pull of the liquid poison, and I wasn't sure if it would be healthy for me to partake. Not just in the physical, but in the emotional part of her. She was already bringing out feelings in me that I hadn't even been aware existed. And now that I'd tasted her and held her in my arms, I couldn't think of anyone else. It seemed obvious to me that one addiction was clearly taking the place of another.

"Hey." She spoke aloud again, this time softly like she was coddling a baby.

"You're beautiful." I didn't know if I'd get another chance to tell her, and I wasn't going to let her go without doing so. I leaned back, giving her room to put her blouse back on if she wanted.

She wasn't having any of it. Hooking each of her legs onto the back of my thighs, she brought me down to her again. This time, I waited as she took the lead. Her hands rubbed my fevered skin, until she lifted my shirt up and over my head. Our gazes never lost contact as she dropped my shirt beside the couch.

"I don't ever want to see your body look like this again." Her nails scraped gently across my bruised chest. "I can't do it, Conner."

"I know." I kissed her trembling lips.

"No." She stopped me by gently pushing on my chest. "I physically can't do it. It reminds me of something I hate." I quirked an eyebrow at her choice of words. "Not *that* kind of hate." She rolled her eyes. "*Real* hate, the kind where self-loathing is the positive adjective to describe what I felt about myself. There was a time where . . ."

"Where what?" I lifted myself up on my elbows, giving her my full attention. As much as I wasn't one for small talk, I hung on her every word.

"Where I didn't care what happened to me. Where I spent time shadow-boxing my other half. I saw that in you—inside the cage earlier. I promised myself I'd never be weak like that again. Promise me you'll do the same." Her hand pushed harder, demanding my vow.

"I promise," I whispered.

Lifting my pinky up to hers, we both kissed each other's skin, giving the promise more weight. It felt like I'd just sold my soul to an angel. All the insecurities I had only a few moments ago, to the ones that had haunted me for years—they all seemed to disappear in that moment. As if my promise to her meant more than my swearing to never quit again as a fighter. It was as if I'd just pledged to be the best version of myself to me—and her. So much so, that even though we fell asleep in each other's arms without making love, I'd never been more fulfilled.

I loved her, and I'd never love anyone else.

CHAPTER 10
WILLOW

"WHERE ARE ALL YOUR UNDERWEAR?" I asked, setting a tray of grapes and cheese on the coffee table in front of Conner. "I've done two loads of laundry, and haven't come across so much as a pair of boxers." Doing his laundry hadn't been high on my list of things to keep me busy, but I found myself in the small wash-room, doing it anyway.

He shrugged. "Don't have any."

"You don't have any?" Not bothering in the least to keep my eyes away from his package, I glanced down at the bulge in his sweat pants. "None?"

He chuckled, wiping moisture away from his eye, like I'd just sent him into a fit of laughter, performing the latest comic relief routine. "Nope."

"Why are you laughing?" I picked the trash up from his last snack of peanut butter crackers. "What's so funny about me asking if you have underwear? I mean normal people wear underwear, especially ones who, you know, have that much junk." I nodded to his mid-section.

"I don't like being constricted." He grinned and shrugged, wincing at the movement in his shoulder.

"So, you don't wear anything under your shorts when you're fighting?" Not that I was looking there during his fights, but everything always appeared to be in place.

"I have to wear a cup when I fight."

I smiled at his admission. So, he wore them sometimes. Glancing at my watch, I knew I needed to leave early to beat the morning traffic. "I have that interview to get to. Do you need anything before I go?"

"Already?"

"Yeah, because bills, you know?" I winked and grabbed my purse off the end table.

"Kiss me."

I smiled and leaned down to give him what he wanted. I'd planned on doing it anyway, but I liked that he thought about it before I did.

Luckily, being prepared was my middle name, and leaving early had been a good call. I only passed one minor accident and witnessed two road-rage incidents, which fortunately sped past me.

I checked my phone as I pulled into the parking lot. Normally, I wasn't a nervous person, but for some reason, I kept thinking I had the time wrong for the interview. As I walked inside the trendy coffee house, my gaze landed on an attractive brunette in a navy-blue dress that looked as if it costed more than my last month's rent. She smiled, letting me know she'd been expecting me.

"Thank you for meeting me at such a late notice," she said as I approached the table. "I had planned on coming to the city next week, but those plans changed. I'm Dana." She pulled her laptop out of the case on the table.

"Willow. And, it was no problem at all. Thank you for meeting with me."

I had no idea what the advertised freelance position entailed. The only information the ad had given suggested it was for a women's magazine. For all I knew, it could be writing reviews for vibrators. And given that I'd used a total of one my entire life, I wouldn't exactly consider myself qualified.

"I have seventy-five magazines that I contract for. No topics are off the table. So, if your writing is good, and I mean good," she leveled me with a look, "then I'd sub-contract your piece for a certain amount of money. Each job pays different."

"Is this something I can live off of?" I wasn't sure how she'd take my question, but I needed a reliable source of income.

"Sure. If your writing capabilities are decent, that is. I have several writers who write for multiple magazines. It can be a lucrative career, but like I said, you must be good. People have to respond to your style. They need to be interested in what you have to say, or why you have a certain perspective on whatever topic you are writing about."

"Okay, this sounds fun. What do I need to do to convince you to hire me?" No sense in beating around the bush. Plus, I could work from home? Count me in.

"I'll give you three topics today. The directions are on the paper," she said, handing me two copies, then promptly typing on her computer. "These need to be completed, edited, and submitted to me within two weeks. My contact information is at the top of the page."

I glanced down at the paper:

Politics for Millennials
Diets that Actually Work
Boyfriends vs. Star Boys

Okay. These were subjects I could have an opinion on. But could I impress her with my bullshitting capabilities? Sure, why not. I could bullshit with the best of them, especially from behind a computer screen.

It was settled then. I'd go home and kill it.

No pressure.

I answered a few more questions, handed over my resume, and chatted about some of her favorite places to visit while she was in town. It was formal, but I didn't mind. It was a job interview after all, and being able to get groceries next month would help keep me afloat. I finished my coffee as she politely advised me that she had another appointment.

The next three weeks passed quicker than normal because I was enjoying my job. I liked it so much, I found myself working longer than the eight hours Dana required. I hadn't seen her since my interview, but she stayed in contact with me weekly through email. She seemed relatively easy-going, but distant. That was cool. I had enough friends, and Conner kept my mind occupied during my down time.

I'd been so caught up in my other job, I hadn't realized what writing could afford me in terms of freedom. I was shit at writing lengthy pieces, but as I gained more experience, I learned short, colorful, opinionated works were my sweet spot. I had been forwarded a couple of emails praising my wit and ability to connect with the readers from the magazines. Those words of encouragement were huge for my confidence. I found, as time passed, I was getting more comfortable and poised, knowing that someone was listening to what I had to say.

"Conner!" I yelled from his living room.

"Back here," he answered from his bedroom.

I stepped inside his room to find him taking clothes out of his top drawer and piling them on the floor. I knew him too well to assume he was spring cleaning. "What are you doing?"

"Making room for you."

His words stopped me in my tracks. We'd never discussed making room for me. "For?"

He shrugged, as he threw the clothes in his hand into the bottom drawer. "If you ever need it, it's there."

He wasn't making a big deal out of it, so I decided not to either—at least on the outside. Conner and I had become relaxed around one another, but talking about the future hadn't been something we'd done. Typically, he seemed okay with going day to day, and I was too. Except sometimes, when he showed me he wasn't typical, I wanted to melt into a puddle at his feet.

"Sometimes, I really hate you," I whispered as I ran my palm from his naked shoulder down to the center of his back. His muscles tightened at my touch. It was as if I had the secret code for unlocking pure delight in his body. Physically, he might have been considered intimidating to most people, but to me, he was perfect. I'd spent hours tracing every scar, every imperfection, trying to massage them into his skin so they'd disappear. Even though he didn't know my intentions, he sighed and relaxed each time. His demeanor transformed under my fingertips, and it made me feel like Houdini.

I took it upon myself to hook the sides of his shorts with my thumbs and pull them down slowly, so that he would get that I was in control. I kicked them aside once they reached his feet, and continued to massage his back. I placed both my palms on his shoulders and rubbed all the way down to his ass. His breathing deepened—almost hypnotic, and I reveled in the fact that he was so turned on by such sweet, simple contact.

He turned so that we were facing each other. "I hate you too."

I stood a foot shorter than Conner and undoubtedly, my gaze landed on his muscular stomach. Internally, I counted each ab as I lightly scratched my nails across them, stunned at how toned they were. He tensed, muscles bulging and stretching across his tanned skin as if my nails were swords and one wrong move would end him. I held my smile inside and continued my path of lustrous wonderment. I was in love with his body. The shape of him brought out feelings I'd never felt before. Appreciation. Lust. Power.

His thickness aroused, creating something inside me I couldn't nail down. Obviously, he was fit, but it seemed to me I was attracted to how solid he was. The breadth of his shoulders reminded me of a Balk Eagle's wingspan. His arms were dense enough to pick up a refrigerator. His chest was full, and even though it was hard as steel, it was soft enough to make me feel safe when he cradled me with a hug. His thighs were full and strapping. The dark curly hairs on them were perfectly proportioned, all the way down to his ankles.

I ran my hand down his right hip, pressing harder as I reached his powerful thigh. His muscle flexed under my fingers, causing me to squeeze harder. I paused to look up at him. His body wasn't the only thing that was tense. His heated observation pinned me, stopping me in my tracks. For someone who hadn't said a word, his features spoke volumes.

I held my hand in place, while staring at the crease of his brow and his pursed lips. It was obvious he didn't like taking things slow. I could not only see, but truly feel, it was taking a lot of effort for him to hold back. Forcing him out of his comfort zone enthralled me. It made me want to make him wait forever.

I winked at him, then continued my soft assault. "Patience, grasshopper."

"I'm about to show *you* some patience."

Normally, I would have laughed at him mentally and *physically* struggling, but I was too focused. Nothing could have broken my concentration in that moment. I wanted to bring him to his knees. Walking in on him doing something so thoughtful had turned my insides to complete mush. Inviting me into his personal space had been the sweetest gesture and it made me happy. I'd never been in a relationship so selfless. It was liberating.

Going to my knees, I traced the skin around his stomach, then down to his pubic bone. His length had grown twice its size. Desire shot through me, as I geared up to continue my attempt at creating a moment between us—one that neither of us had ever experienced. Not in the act itself, but in the crackle of fire that existed between us, knowing once we *went* there, there would be no containing the inferno.

I'd never experienced that level of passion with anyone before. Attraction, sure. But not feeling like if I didn't do everything I could to show him how much I cared about him, I would be failing somehow. I wanted nothing but pure bliss to circle his mind as I showed him what a joke our mutual hatred for each other was. I loved him. I loved him as much as I loved myself, and that scared the shit out of me as much as it elated me.

Giving him all of me, I took him in my mouth and swirled my tongue.

"Damn, woman!" He groaned.

We'd spent the last three weeks talking and fooling around like a couple of teenagers, but never taking our physical relationship all the way. I knew he was waiting on me.

Well, I was ready.

Strong hands gripped the sides of my head, his large fingers thrusting through the strands of my hair haphazardly, nearly ripping pieces out at the root. Pain fizzled into pleasure the wilder he got with his movements. I was driving him mad physically, and he was driving me insane emotionally. It was as if we were professional dancers, pushing and pulling like a perfect magnet, our movements comple-menting one another.

My heart fluttered as he pushed his hands under my armpits and lifted me so high, my stomach was level with his mouth. He walked steady to the bed, placing kisses on the patch of skin peeking out from my raised shirt. Heat flooded my body. As hot as I'd been while giving him pleasure, nothing compared to the thrilling sensation of his lips on my skin.

He grunted as he pulled my pants off, before tugging my shirt over my head. My bra lay haphazardly, causing my breasts to come out of the cups. With one hand, he reached behind me and unclasped the hook. His face was contorted, almost looking pained. There was some-thing so poetic in his reactions. Like he was spilling his guts—his deepest thoughts—to me through visual expression. It was how he did most of his communication, and I'd gotten to know him so well, it worked for us. It worked for me.

His eyes softened as he took in my bare breasts. Leaning in slightly, he pulled one of them into his mouth. Bursts of color shot behind my eyelids from the pleasure. I couldn't imagine anything feeling better than Conner kissing the life out of my body.

I was wrong.

Lifting his weight from me, he continued his path of feather-light kisses down my body. My stomach dipped of its own accord; my muscles were quite content on playing hide-and-seek from his tongue.

Bringing my knees up, I squeezed my legs around him, feeling like I would crack one of his ribs as he peppered kisses along the top of my pubic hair. He pulled my panties to the side and his tongue dipped into my center. I lifted my hips off the bed, searching for more, but he didn't give it to me. He teased me as if he enjoyed watching me melt right before his eyes.

Kissing my hip bone, Conner took one side of my panties into his mouth and tugged a few times, bringing one side down to my thigh. Then made his way back up to the other side, only to do the same thing. The whole time we'd been working our way up to making love, he'd taken control of the physical side of things, but had left the emotional part up to me. Even with his calculated movements, at every pause, I knew he was silently waiting for me to give consent.

And I gave it to him, with a fevered sigh of anticipation.

Growling, he discarded my panties behind him and climbed up my body, until we were lined up seamlessly. "You're perfect."

I grinned at his sweetness. "So are you." I brought his cheek to my lips and placed a barely-there kiss at the bottom of his jaw. Feeling my way across his face, I traced his lips with my thumb, following its path blindly with my mouth.

Even when he opened the side drawer for a condom, he didn't break our rhythm. Within seconds, he prepared himself and thrust into me.

I gasped, as the tiniest pain shot from the exact spot where our bodies connected. It was gone as soon as I felt it, but it still surprised me. After what felt like a needle prick, pleasure surged through me, as if melting me from the inside. My legs relaxed, sweeping down the length of his legs, my toes sinking into every piece of skin they could reach.

"You okay?" he asked gruffly.

"Yes. Please don't stop." I reached behind me, grasping for anything that would anchor me. I didn't want to risk losing any space between us.

He lifted my right leg, kissed my calf, then moved my leg directly in front of him. His hips resumed the pumping motion, but his face was curious—almost examining. A chill ran up my back as I watched him watch me, like he had to know what I felt in that position. Moments later, he brought my leg to the other side of his head and draped it over his shoulder.

I cried out with each movement, louder each time, experiencing unadulterated euphoria as our bodies melded so well together, I felt like we were one.

"I can't get close enough to you." He leaned forward, my leg the only thing stopping him from pressing into me completely.

At his words, my defenses shattered. Feeling like I was suffocating under the weight of my emotions, I attempted to quicken our pace from underneath him. I was in limbo, wanting our connection to never end, yet clawing to reach the top of an invisible mountain.

I pushed into him as hard as I could, trying to get all I could from the last moments. His body drilled into mine with such delicious force, I screamed out and let go of everything; a wave of ecstasy raced from my core to my limbs. He grunted and tensed up from his own release, before sinking into me contentedly.

Silence fell around us like a blanket. It probably would have been awkward with anyone else, but with Conner, it was a moment of clarity. We were on the same page, neither of us confessing what we were feeling, but knowing without a doubt, the same thoughts and sentiments were buzzing through both of our minds, bodies, and souls at the same time.

When he rolled off me and to the side, I reached for him. Even though I hadn't been able to breathe before, I didn't want to lose the closeness. Snuggling up to his side, he caressed my shoulder. Goose bumps broke out over my skin, but I didn't reach for the comforter. I basked in the chill, knowing he'd caused it.

"I think it's fair to let you know I've spent years trying to become who I want to be," I whispered.

"We all do."

I nodded. I had issues, but he had them too. I wanted to know his every secret, and what had kept him so strong during his stint in prison. I wanted him to know I was a work in progress, but I'd never give up.

I bit my bottom lip and raised slightly, so I could look into his eyes. "Full disclosure?"

"Okay."

"I'm not proud of most of the things I've done. I've made horrible decision after horrible decision. One of the reasons I'm here, in this town, is because I wanted to make a new start."

He continued rubbing my shoulder, concentrating on a single spot. I was sure he didn't realize he was even doing it. "I get that," he finally answered.

"I let other people influence me, and broke my back to do anything

I could to make them happy. I put anything and anyone before myself."

"Happiness is an inside job."

"It is. I've learned that since then, but—"

"I got you, babe. You can tell me the worst thing imaginable, and I'd still feel the same way about you. Nothing you could say will ever change that."

I took a deep breath, then reached for the sheet and blanket at the end of his bed. Something inside me needed a shield. "Overdosing wasn't what made me want to change my life. You know, when you live at the lowest level imaginable, it's hard to see the top of that mountain. But rehab changed me. Therapy made me see what I had to lose. It literally took another human being to tell me how much I mattered before I believed it."

I expected him to respond sooner. Instead, I watched his Adam's apple bob up and down multiple times, as he swallowed the words he'd started to speak, over and over, yet never did. I feared my admission would change his perception of me. I knew from experience that even though no one ever wanted to be judgmental, sometimes as humans, we couldn't help it. The only thing we ever had to go on was someone's past, because we didn't know the future yet.

"I promise I'll never let you feel that low again." He kissed the side of my head. "As long as I'm breathing, you won't ever feel worthless again."

I smiled and sat up. I crossed my legs, readying myself for our not-so-pillow-talk.

He followed my lead and pressed his back to the headboard. The sheet just barely covered him. "I don't think about it when I'm around you. The alcohol," he admitted.

As good as his words made me feel, I knew from experience you couldn't put your addiction in someone else's hands. It could never be up to me, because he had free will. At any given moment, he could change his future, without so much as asking my opinion; and if he ever got into a vulnerable headspace, my opinion wouldn't matter anyway. Addiction was selfish like that.

"I'm glad you're not suffering. Have you ever thought about AA or therapy?"

"Nah. They had a program in prison. I don't know." He brought his arm up behind his head lost in thought. "It wasn't like people were there because they wanted to be, you know?"

I nodded in understanding. "Well, I'm here for you. Whatever you need, Conner."

He leaned forward and pulled me onto his lap. "Come here."

In silence, we held each other. Listened to one another's heart beats and shallow breaths. Even with all the sharing we'd done, we both knew no matter what came tomorrow, nothing could change how perfect tonight had been.

CHAPTER 11
CONNER

"DAMN, man. We're only going to be gone for three days," Steele chuckled, putting our bags in the back of his Jeep.

"Shut the fuck up," I mumbled from around Willow's lips. She'd driven up to the gym just to say goodbye.

"No need to fight, boys." Willow pulled away from me and winked. "Call me when you get a chance."

"Will do." I swatted her ass one last time, and jumped into the passenger's side, ready to roll.

Steele managed the side streets with ease and didn't speak up until we hit the freeway. "So, you and Willow?"

I hadn't made an announcement, but it wasn't exactly a secret. "You knew about it already."

"Well, yeah, I mean I knew you guys were dating, but I didn't realize it was serious."

"It's serious."

He chuckled and shook his head. I wasn't sure what he found so funny about it, and I didn't care enough to ask. I closed my eyes and thought about the perfect woman I'd just left in the parking lot. I never imagined I could experience the kind of happiness Willow gave me—not after the accident. For years, I'd only been concerned about making it day to day. The future had never occurred to me. It wasn't something tangible.

But now—even though I wasn't sure what was going to happen, I knew I wanted her there. With me. Hence, my reminiscing about not wanting to leave her behind on my way to Las Vegas with Steele. I would have gone, regardless, to support my buddy in his fight, but I had a second agenda in mind as well.

Meeting Richard Fuller, the CEO of the AFL was an opportunity Steele wasn't going to let me pass up. He'd been talking me up for the last couple of months, trying to get Richard to come to one of my fights. He'd even sent him a couple of fight tapes. Steele said the CEO was interested, but was firm in the fact that I needed more experience. I didn't disagree, and agreed with Steele that Mr. Fuller and I needed a face to face. As Steele put it, it wouldn't hurt my chances.

Once arriving in Vegas, Steele and I stayed low key. It was his fight night. If he was anything like me, he didn't need me up his ass every two minutes asking if he was ready to fight. Not to mention, the fight was a live pay-per-view event, which meant money was being made per minute. There was more pressure involved with this fight.

I could tell he was antsy. He'd only ever fought Mackle once before, but that was two years ago. I hadn't actually watched their previous match until recently. Mackle was a squirrely little shit, but in the fighting profession, those were the ones you had to watch out for.

The tenth time Steele walked out onto the balcony, I decided to speak up. "You all right?"

"Yeah."

"You sure about that?"

He took a sip of his water. "I haven't said anything because I'm not sure yet, but I'm considering retirement."

"Why?" He hadn't mentioned a word to me about quitting.

"Dude, my knees hurt. My back is fucked up. My neck aches more often than not. I'm thirty-five. I'm not as young as I used to be, you know?"

I nodded, understanding what he was saying, but still shocked. "I get it. Just don't think about that shit today. Not on a fight night. Get this win, then we'll start planning your funeral. Okay, old man?"

"Funeral? You're a real prick." He grinned, but I could tell he wasn't done thinking about it. He threw his backpack over his shoulder and started for the door, letting me know it was go time.

Walking into the arena was surreal. I'd never been to a fight so anticipated before. The crowds were already forming outside. I got a small glimpse of what it would be like if I were to go pro, and instead of being excited, I found myself second-guessing the whole process. It was almost as if seeing behind the scenes for the first time shocked my system. It terrified me more than anything, and I didn't like the uncertainty of it all. Not to mention, there were cameras in his face every time he turned around, and a constant stream of people wanting autographs. It was too busy for me.

Steele introduced me to a gaggle of people—from the guys who set up the cage, to the PR people for the league. I even met a few professional fighters who were there for support, but during those interactions, my mind kept reverting back to my insecurities. The more I thought about them, the more I wanted to bust out of Vegas and return to Boston.

"Hey, man. Good to meet you." Jesse Jamison shook my hand.

He was the best fighter who'd ever been in the league. A true legend. He had more wins under his belt than anyone who'd come before him, and everyone who'd fought long past his day in the cage. He'd also gone undefeated in his career, which was an accomplishment in and of itself. He was the fastest. The fiercest. The most incredible ground fighter there was. Not much impressed me, but he sure as hell did.

"Same." I nodded as I glanced from him to Steele. I had a feeling my buddy was still preoccupied from our earlier conversation. He was more quiet than normal.

"You ready to kick a little ass, Steele?" Jamison smiled, showing us his gold tooth. "Mackle told Hinder he'd have you tapping in three rounds."

"Three? I plan on shutting this down in two." Steele slammed his locker, placing a roll of tape on the table.

"We'll see, my man." He turned his attention to me, while Steele continued to prep. "Steele tells me you're a hell of a fighter."

"I do okay."

He chuckled, and so did the rest of the guys milling around. "Are you interested in fighting at this level?" he asked.

"Not sure," I said, my head leaned all the way back to inspect the huge ceiling.

"He is. He just doesn't know it yet," Steele replied.

"Cool." Jesse's voice had a hint of sarcasm to it, but I ignored it.

Just a couple of minutes before, he'd seemed like a decent dude, but because I wasn't gung-ho over being a part of their club, he was quickly becoming an asshole.

"Victory party at Glow. My treat." Jesse bumped knuckles with Steele and left us alone, taking his entourage with him.

"He's cool. Just likes to show off sometimes," Steele said, taking in my reaction to his friend.

"I bet," I said dryly. *My favorite.*

He shook his head, as the trainer walked in to wrap his hands. I sat quietly, allowing Steele the time to gather his thoughts, and work through whatever nerves he'd been feeling prior. He hadn't exactly been anxious, but he wasn't his hunky-dory self either. He'd never shown any signs of weakness during our sparring sessions, and I'd never so much as seen him take an ice bath due to soreness. Hell, at his gym, he always seemed perfectly in control of every situation. I wondered if he'd prepared mentally, like he always told me to do.

I wanted to mention it to him, but figured saying something would let him know I noticed something was off, which had the potential of making matters worse. So, I kept my mouth shut. He was the professional. I knew he'd pull through.

I left just before it was time for him to enter the cage. I walked the long tunnel alone, taking in my surroundings as I tried to clear my mind of everything not involving his fight. Entering the arena, I took my place just to the right of the cage and his corner. As the lights dimmed, and Steele entered, the crowd lurched to their feet, cheering over the music blaring through the speakers. His coach, who'd been with him from the beginning, talked him up, giving him direction just before Mackle entered. I watched intently, hoping like hell Steele had been able to get his mind straight.

Once the signal had been given by the referee, Mackle went at Steele full-force, throwing three punches in the first two minutes that should have knocked him out. Steele stumbled after the last one, but luckily, it was time to meet at the corners.

"He's fast. He's handing out strikes like it's Halloween candy," his trainer said as he wiped Steele's face.

"I got it. It took me a minute to decipher his technique."

"Then stop taking them, dumbass. Cover yourself. You're going to get knocked out before you even get a chance to take him to the ground."

I hadn't ever been so worked up over a fight. Not even one of my own. Watching my buddy struggle didn't sit well with me. I wanted to go fight for him. He was sluggish, and his feet appeared heavy. Mackle was quick, and he was striking twice as much as Steele. Granted, that could have caused him to tire out faster, but taking punches, one right after the other, would affect anyone—Steele was no exception.

There were times where I thought Steele was going to lose, and I wasn't the only person. The tension in his corner was so thick, you could have cut it with a knife. Add in the crowd, and it was almost too much to bear. Every punch he took, every kick of Mackle's that made contact, pissed me off.

Finally, in round three, Steele swept Mackle's legs out from under him in a takedown. Relief rushed through my body, knowing that he had him. Mackle's eyes bulged out, his face blood-red, as Steele squeezed tighter. Just before Mackle lost consciousness, he tapped.

Jesus. That was a close call.

Afterward, it had taken Steele a full thirty minutes to sign autographs at the back door, before we were finally on our way to the victory party Jamison was throwing. Honestly, I wasn't quite up for the party scene, but after the effort my best friend had just put down, we had to celebrate somehow. Not to mention, the pay day he'd received. I would have felt like a complete jackass not acknowledging his win.

"Welcome! Welcome, boys. Make yourselves comfortable. The ladies will be here in a moment." A middle-aged, balding man in a black suit led us to our table.

"Ladies?" I asked. I wasn't a pussy by any means, but pissing my girlfriend off over a couple of cage bunnies wasn't something I was trying to do.

"I got us some strippers!" Jamison put his fist in the air.

"Damn." I grimaced, knowing it wasn't a good idea.

"I don't give a fuck who shows up," Steele said. "I'm getting drunk. I'm getting laid. And I don't want to remember either of those things when I wake up tomorrow."

I couldn't be the downer of the group, so I let it ride. I'd just keep to myself, like I usually did, and all would be well.

It will all be—

"Payne!"

Fuck.

I would've recognized that voice anywhere. Simone. And from the looks of it, she was already lit. The straps on her dress were falling down her arms, and her hair was a stringy mess. The last thing I wanted to deal with was an intoxicated Simone. I couldn't believe I hadn't thought of her showing up. She was a cage bunny after all; a popular one at that. Of course she'd show for a live event.

I looked up, just as she planted her ass on my lap. Getting ready to push her off, somebody bumped into me from the side, and almost knocked two dancers to the floor. Flashes from the side caught my attention. I hated cellphones. I hated social media. And I didn't care for paparazzi either. Especially when I had to run from a past I was ashamed of.

Once I found my footing, I jumped up. All I could think about was which photos would end up where. It had only been a matter of seconds, but I was smart enough to know a picture spoke a thousand words.

"What's your problem, Con?" Simone slurred.

Hearing her nickname for me grossed me out. "Don't call me that."

"Oh, I see. You got in the journalist's pants and now you're too good for me?" She was smiling, knowing she had my attention at the mention of Willow.

"What do you know about the journalist?"

We had an audience. The music was drowning out most of our

conversation, but anyone standing near us could hear. In the VIP section, that still left a lot of ears, given it was such a small area.

"Enough." Her perfectly manicured brow rose as she tried to bait me.

I cocked my head to the side. She was lying. She didn't know Willow.

I'd told Willow about her one night, when we'd talked about our exes. I admitted that Simone was the closest thing I had to an ex. I explained who she was, and what she did for a living. Willow knew what cage bunnies were because she'd seen them before. Luckily, her path hadn't crossed with Simone's yet.

Simone knew how to get under my skin, and she knew exactly which buttons to push to get a reaction out of me.

"You're a fucking liar," I spat.

"What am I lying about? I said I knew enough about her." She took two gulps of whatever she had in her glass.

I glanced to either side of me, wanting to get the confrontation over with. But not before I found out what her angle was. "What do you want, Simone? I'm not in the mood for this shit."

She was manipulative enough for me to recognize I had something to fear. Our fallout hadn't been pretty, and she was petty. She'd try and pay me back. Normally, I wouldn't have even entertained her drunk ass, but her bringing Willow into the mix, changed things.

Before she could answer, I felt my phone vibrate in my jeans. Something inside my gut told me it was Willow. I wanted to answer, but I knew I wouldn't be able to hear her inside the club. Plus, I wasn't done with Simone yet. I wanted to know what her end game was.

"You. I want you," she said.

"Not going to happen. In this lifetime, or the next."

Staring at her, all disheveled and wasted, only made me hate myself more for going there in the first place. You get what you pay for, and a cage bunny was worth pennies compared to what I had at home.

She glanced down to the main floor of the club. "Someone was asking about you earlier."

Taking her lead, I peered over the rails, and there in a crowd of hundreds, stood Mikey Godwin. My eyes widened, seeing him for the first time in over two years. Shocked, my feet were moving before I even had time to think about what I was going to do once I reached him.

Anger seeped out of my pores like beads of sweat. I huffed twice, trying to stabilize my breathing. It didn't help.

Mikey had been a fellow inmate in the state penitentiary, and he loved picking fights with me behind bars. Once, I kicked his ass the old school way, without a weapon, even though he'd been able to smuggle a pair of brass knuckles inside, hoping to use them on me. I'd had to watch my back every day after that. I never knew what his problem was with me, and honestly, I hadn't cared back then.

I took the stairs two at a time, until I reached the club floor. Black eyes peered out from behind one of the pillars; a sinister smile crossing the face of my prison enemy. His appearance hadn't changed much, with the exception of a few added gold teeth.

"What do you want?" I asked.

He was alone, from what I could see. I glanced behind me once more just to be sure.

"Payne, old buddy. How are ya?" His hand reached up to touch my shoulder, but I dodged it. My instincts heightened, creating a fight or flight gut check. I knew his reason for being at the club had nothing to do with seeing how I was doing.

"What the fuck do you want?" I asked through clenched teeth.

He grinned. "We've got some shit to settle."

"No, we don't." Heat pulsed through my body. My fingers tingled, itching to hit him. To make him disappear.

"We'll see about that."

I stepped up to him, pushing my forehead into his, applying just enough pressure for him to get my point. "Leave me the fuck alone. Don't come near me again."

"Damn, boy." He chuckled. "You're tense. Guess all that time you spent behind bars made you all paranoid and shit."

"I'm not fucking with you. Our last tussle will seem like a middle school fight if I ever see you around again," I threatened.

I turned to leave, and he pushed me in the back. It was barely a nudge, but I felt it. I faced him, ready to stomp a mud hole in his ass, when Steele stepped in between us. He placed his palm on my chest. His eyes widened just a hair, and I knew he could feel my heart racing. My breaths were short and shallow. At best, fear was clouding my judgement where Mikey was concerned. Not fear of him, but fear that my past had finally caught up with me. Obviously, he wasn't going to leave me alone. His subtle, but stern nudge in the back told me as much.

Steele stepped up to Mikey. "Dude, what's your problem?"

Mikey shrugged, like he had no idea what Steele was talking about. "Don't got one," he said, and stepped back, raising both hands in the air.

Steele looked back at me. I closed my eyes, knowing I had everything to lose. I stepped back too. "A simple misunderstanding. We're good."

Steele wasn't buying it. "Man—"

"I'm good. I swear. Just tired. I'll meet you back at the hotel."

Steele squinted in question, but relented. "All right. Holler at me if you need me."

"Seriously," I was already walking backward, "go celebrate."

I had planned on hailing a cab, but didn't see one as I exited the club, so I began walking. I needed to burn some energy off anyway. Crazy memories slammed through my mind like a flip book. All the truths—and some of the lies. I couldn't form a complete thought, feeling like such a fraud. Why was it so hard to move on? To overcome what I had been in hopes of becoming someone I wanted to be.

After a few blocks, I remembered that Willow had called. I needed to hear her voice. It wouldn't quieten the insecurities.

"Where are you?" she questioned without greeting me. She sounded pissed.

"I'm walking down the strip," I answered honestly.

"Who are you with?"

"I'm by myself, why?"

"Really? Because I just saw pictures online where you were in a dark club with that skank, Simone, on your lap."

My stomach sank. It hadn't even been thirty minutes, and already the pictures had gone viral. Every fear I had in attempting to go professional was happening in one moment. A moment that kept getting worse as the night wore on.

"That's not what it looked like," I started to explain.

"Are you drunk?" she asked. "You've been drinking, haven't you?"

I hadn't even realized I'd stopped walking. I just stood there, on the side of the street, surrounded by bright lights and a million people I didn't know, feeling completely alone. I swallowed my denial, unable to speak. Out of all the things Willow and I had confided in each other, all the messed-up shit I had told her about my life, she didn't think I could manage one weekend in Las Vegas without throwing in the towel?

My eyes focused on the homeless man to my right. He had no shoes on, only socks. His jacket had four holes in it, and the toboggan he wore was bright green. If I hadn't seen him move, I would have thought he was dead. To the right of his thigh were two bottles of whiskey. Dark gold, and unopened.

The sounds of the night flooded my brain, and in that split second, I couldn't hear Willow doubt me anymore. It occurred to me that being accused of being weak only made me want to prove her right.

I hung up, not even answering her, and made my way to the corner. I pulled two twenties out of my wallet and placed them in the homeless man's lap. He didn't respond, and by the time he reacted to the money, I'd already bent forward and picked up the bottles, not even bothering to ask him if I could buy them from him. He didn't decline. I wouldn't have cared if he did. My mind was made up.

The rush I got while walking away from the vagrant should have worried me, but it didn't, because I knew all too well that once the adrenaline wore off, I'd crash like I always had. But for some reason, it wasn't something I focused on. It was probably because it wasn't the high I was chasing this time. It was the emptiness. I wanted to get so lost, that even I couldn't find my way out.

My past had caught up to me, and it only made me want to disappear even more. All I'd needed was the one person I'd given the power to believe in me to doubt me. Within half an hour, the past decade crashed down on me, threatening to swallow me whole. Add in the fact that Willow had zero faith in me—it wasn't as hard as I'd hoped it to be to let go. It should have been, but it wasn't.

I held the bottles close to my chest, like they were going to grow legs and try to escape my grasp. I walked with purpose, until I saw the bright lights of our hotel lit up perfectly in the night sky. It may as well have been a blinking red arrow saying, *This Way*.

I kept to myself, not making eye contact with the people who walked past me. Head down, I took the elevator all the way up to my room, still reeling from my conversation with Willow. As much as I didn't want to think about it, her words overtook every thought I had. She had disappointed me. She'd let me down. I'd mistakenly thought our relationship was solid. I hadn't realized she thought she was the only one strong enough to hold it up.

Crossing the threshold of my hotel room made me feel like I vanished into another world. I turned and bolted the door shut. Not that I thought I'd be hearing from Steele, but better safe than sorry. I took a seat in the chair next to the window. I peeked out the partially closed curtains, not taking anything in at first.

As much as I knew I was making a mistake, all I could focus on was giving Willow what she wanted. What she expected. Going back home and groveling, basically working my ass off to prove my innocence wasn't what I wanted to do. I didn't want to ever do that again. It seemed that had been my entire life up until this point. Trying to show my mom I wasn't just a fuck-up who did everything I could to hurt her. Displaying remorse to a family I didn't know or proving to Steele, and anybody in a suit, that I had what it took inside the cage to make a career in a profession I hadn't trained my whole life for.

Turning to the only comfort I was willing to seek for the night, I opened the first bottle and took a swig. Fighting back tears, I continued drinking until I forgot about it all.

CHAPTER 12
WILLOW

I TRIED CALLING Conner four times, and sent him ten text messages, before I gave in and texted Steele.

Conner had hung up on me; hadn't even apologized. At first, I was angry. How could he expect me not to be upset by another girl sitting on his lap, especially when said girl was his ex? Well, he'd assured me they'd never been exclusive, but still. She'd been his bed mate whenever he needed the warmth, and she was a cage bunny to top it off. Which meant she had very little self-respect. In my mind, anyhow. The point was, Simone wouldn't give two shits if Conner had a girlfriend. But she also wasn't the one in our relationship, which was the main reason I didn't hold her responsible. My boyfriend should have had more respect for me than that.

I gave up on trying to get a hold of him once Steele texted me back and told me he was fine. Conner was good, and had gone back to his hotel room. I tried not to imagine him going back to the room with her even though I couldn't guarantee it. But I had more pride in myself than to ask Steele about the whole situation.

I honestly didn't think Conner would ever cheat on me, but with proof circulating the internet of another girl sitting comfortably on his lap, I couldn't help but fear the unknown. What happened in Vegas, stayed in Vegas, or say they say. He was there. She was there. And I wasn't there.

I hated picturing it. I hated imagining them in a club together, surrounded by people partying, with the alcohol flowing. Conner's weakness. I wiped a lone tear from my eye. I'd only drive myself insane thinking about all the what ifs, if my mind kept wandering in that direction.

Since it was clear I wouldn't be getting the answers I wanted, and believed I deserved, I gave up trying to force him to talk to me, and concentrated on work. Maybe putting my energy into something else would allow me the fortitude to not visualize the worst. Dana had given me certain freedoms with my next articles, since a few of the editors from her biggest clients had requested me specifically for their future assignments.

It helped that the current project I was working on was the world according to women. Dana had some business out of town and had allowed me to choose my own topic. She said she'd shop it around once she was back in her office. For once, I was appreciative of her aloof personality. Luckily, I didn't need much brain power to get a good hook going. I wouldn't have been able to concentrate on a topic that would take much energy, because emotionally, I was spent.

It had been a while since I had felt so off balance. I prided myself in being centered most of the time. It was one of the greatest gifts I'd been given during my stint at rehab. The ability to internally ground myself. But I couldn't help certain fears in my abilities, considering I had *one* fallout with the man I loved, and suddenly I felt like I didn't know which way was up.

The whole thing seemed tragic somehow. I wasn't sure how we'd gone from me wanting to stay at his house more often than my own, to us not even speaking.

Two days. One picture. And a whole lot of doubt.

I had no clue how to fix it all. I knew I *wanted* to, but at the same time, I was beginning to wonder if it was worth it. It worried me how he had reacted to our conflict. Instead of explaining himself, he'd just walked away at the first sign of trouble. I knew not everyone wanted to talk things out the way I did, but I was disappointed in the fact he didn't try. He could have asked for time, or caught the first flight home because the woman he loved—or *hated*—was upset and needed him to clarify why another woman was touching him. But he did none of those things. He'd done nothing. And that hurt more than anything.

Still in a heartbroken funk the following days, I decided it was time to pay my mom a visit. She didn't have to know I needed her in my moment of hell. I just wanted to be around her, to feel her comfort.

She greeted me in her kitchen. "Hey, sweetie. I was a little surprised you called. I didn't think I'd see you until next weekend."

"You didn't want to see me?" I teased.

"Of course I do! Get over here and give your mother a hug."

Immediately, I relaxed. Not much beat my mother's arms when I felt small. Not that she could solve all of life's problems, but I learned a long time ago that a full embrace from her could get me through most things.

"What's going on?"

I chuckled, not surprised in the least. Nothing got past her. "So, we're just going to jump right to it, then?"

"You're thinner than the last time I saw you, you have bags under your eyes, and you're wearing your glasses rather than your contacts. These are all signs that lead me to believe you have not been taking care of yourself. And yes, as your mother, I demand to know why." She smiled, as if she hadn't just verbally insulted me.

"Let me get some coffee first. This may take a while."

After pouring my elixir, and adding her homemade creamer to my cup, I took a seat next to her at the bar. Taking a sip, I considered my words, but finally gave into the fact that unloading my feelings might help more than it would hurt.

"Remember that guy I mentioned? Conner?"

"Yes."

"Well, he and I have grown close."

"That's wonderful, honey."

Exhaling, I spilled my guts to her like I was a fifteen-year-old girl who'd just gone through her first heartbreak. I was one hundred percent focused on giving her only the details, so that she could give me an unbiased opinion on how to handle it. That lasted for about five minutes. It didn't take but one look from her for me to get completely honest.

I told her how I had entrusted Conner with my deepest secret, and that he'd confided in me as well. I told her how much I cared for him, and that I truly loved him. It wasn't that I didn't know how I felt about him, because I did. But admitting my feelings to someone who wasn't in our circle liberated me somewhat. Saying the words out loud to my closest family member made the relationship real.

"So, you haven't seen him since he returned from Las Vegas?"

"Nope." I'd considered running to his house a thousand times over the past two days, demanding he talk to me, but something always stopped me.

"Willow, if you love him like you claim, you need to talk to him. You need to fix this."

"He won't talk to me. I've tried."

"Have you any idea what caused him to snap? What caused him to hang up on you? That was abrupt, and he never explained what his ex was doing there?" Mom had her hands clasped together and her legs crossed. She looked as if she were interviewing someone to clean her house.

I fought back laughter at the thought, and answered her. "I've had time to think about this. I believe I may have jumped to a conclusion and he took offense to it."

"What conclusion?"

"I accused him of being drunk. That was when he hung up on me."

Her eyes softened, and pity grew in her features. At that moment, I wasn't feeling as confident as I had been just minutes before. "You said he had issues with alcohol?" I nodded. "And you assumed he was relapsing without him confirming it?" She leaned her head to the side.

"It seemed like he was." I grimaced. "His voice was shaky, and did you forget the part about him being in a club with his ex on his lap? He would have had to have been drunk. Nothing else makes sense. He wouldn't have allowed that, if he'd been sober."

"Maybe he would. Maybe something happened right before that picture was taken. Baby girl, you know better than anyone what it feels like to be unfairly judged. It's the main reason you don't live here anymore. You said so yourself." She sighed.

Her words stung. She was right. I'd jumped to conclusions where Conner's addiction was concerned, and I knew from experience sharing that weakness with someone only to have them throw it back in your face the moment shit went south sucked. Which was why, at the end of the day, people like Conner and myself didn't share too often. We didn't want it held against us.

"I think I really messed up, Mom." Tears formed behind my eyes at the revelation. "I'm not sure he'll forgive me."

"He will. If he loves you like you love him, he will. You just have to make him understand that your fear came from a real place. The same place he fears every time he turns his back on drinking. A genuine place where you both know what can happen if either of you give into the one thing that can ruin your lives."

I wiped my tears away and hugged her. It was then a thought occurred to me; I had something Conner didn't have. Support. My mother had been there for me from the beginning. His had not. He made his mistakes, and she left him. Unlike my mother, Conner's mother had chosen her own feelings over his. She selfishly decided to take her disappointment and turn it into resentment, instead of lifting her son up so high that his foundation would take a hurricane to bust. No wonder he'd been swept away.

And here I was, acting like his mother had. I'd jumped to conclusions based on how I felt, never once taking into consideration that I was dealing with someone who, like me, had been bent, broken, and flawed; and that maybe, just listening to what he had to say would have benefited both of us.

When I left my mom's house, I drove straight to Conner's, determined for him to hear me out. Even if he didn't forgive me, I knew I owed him an apology. Whether or not he was flirting with an ex-girlfriend, or if he'd been wasted beyond measure, I had assumed the worst about a situation I knew nothing about. I hadn't trusted him, and that was the bottom line.

I wasn't sure what that said about me. I'd thought the whole time we were connecting, talking, and spending time together, I was slowly learning to believe him—to believe *in* him. But maybe, as much as I wanted to be there mentally, I wasn't. Maybe my experiences would never allow me to feel enough security to give him the benefit of the doubt.

I felt defeated pulling into his driveway. His truck was parked outside the garage, so I parked behind him. Sitting in my car for a few minutes, I attempted to pull myself together. I still wasn't sure what I was going to say to him when I knocked on the door. But I moved without thinking any further, and within seconds, he opened the door and stood back, silently inviting me inside.

We didn't exchange pleasantries. In fact, an awkward silence fell around us as I took a seat on his couch. He followed suit, sitting at the opposite end, facing me. His disposition worried me. He was tense, cold. My showing up had set him on edge. He wasn't calm or confident. He was distant; a million miles away, even though I could have reached out and touched him. What little certainty I had faltered.

I wasn't sure what I had expected. In my mind, I'd sort of figured once I explained what I'd felt when I saw the picture, he would understand why I made the assumption he was drunk. But as he sat there, staring at me like he'd never met me before, I wasn't sure I needed to elaborate anymore. I wasn't exactly convinced there was anything left to fight for.

Timidly, I cleared my throat. "I'm sorry."

I took a risk in the silence, my gaze never wavering from his. He nodded, barely moving, but other than the small gesture, he didn't respond. Out of guilt, I continued.

"I shouldn't have assumed anything. I know that now. I've thought about how I would have felt, if you would have assumed the worst with my past and—I'm sorry, Conner. I don't know why I said it. I don't know why I thought it."

"You said it because you believed it."

"Maybe I did." I shrugged. "But now I understand even if I did believe it, I should have trusted you to do the right thing."

His gaze dropped. He seemed extremely focused on a loose piece of thread from the seam of his leather sofa. Our conversation stalled and I watched him turn the thread over his index finger again and again, while I waited on him to respond.

"Why did you believe it? What have I done to give you the impression the first thing I'd do when I got out of town was get wasted and cheat on you?"

I shook my head hating that we'd ended up in such a cruel place. Only days ago, I thought my life couldn't get any better. I thought all my insecurities were in the past, and I finally had peace with myself, allowing me to have an authentic relationship with someone who could love me the way I wanted. The way I needed.

"I don't know. It was almost impulse. I swear, I've gone back to the moment my phone rang a million times, and every single time, all I can remember is that it hurt so bad. I felt betrayed, and the only thing that made sense was that you had to have been intoxicated. There was no way you would have allowed another girl to be that close to you if you were of sound mind."

He blew out a frustrated breath and rose from the couch. I watched him pace back and forth, considering his next words. It worried me that he had to think so hard on what to say.

"After the fight, we all went to a club to celebrate. I had no idea she would be there. She was wasted and fell on me. It took everything I had not to knock her ass to the floor. She was in my lap for a total of five seconds, but I guess that's all it took." He growled, obviously still frustrated by the incident.

I believed him and wanted so badly to tell him, but I felt like he would take offense.

"You hurt me too, you know. All I wanted was to hear your voice. To have you anchor me when I felt out of sorts, because I was in an environment I didn't want to be in. I only went to the after party for Steele. I wanted to support him, but just like every other time I go to places like that, I felt like crawling out of my skin once I got there."

"I'm so sorry." I stood.

"I've never given someone so much power over me. No one has ever had the ability to hurt me the way you do, because I've never loved anyone like I love you."

"I feel the same way about you. I swear, if I could make you understand that my questioning you had more to do with me than it did you, I would. I don't know how to explain it. I guess old habits die hard, even when you think you've fought through the toughest part of them. I thought I had left those insecurities behind, but at the first sign of trouble, I reverted back to them. And I know I can't take it back."

I grabbed his hand and brought it to my mouth. I kissed his palm and held it over my lips while breathing him in. "I will never doubt you again. Please, accept my apology and know that I will do everything in my power to replace your disappointment with assurance in me—in us. I love you, and I want to be with you."

His lips caught mine in surprise. Moving with fervor, his hands shot up my shirt, hot and needy. I helped him remove my jeans and panties while he walked me back to his bedroom. Need overtook every inch of my body and soul. Need for us to reconnect. Need for him to forgive me. I wanted him to understand that I'd learned something in the process as well. I'd only ever known the superficial parts to love. Lust. Being able to co-exist; trusting the person I thought I loved to hold down a job.

I'd never loved someone the way I loved him, where we'd made it to the nucleus—to the deepest part of the relationship. The part where we both understood we were our own person without the other, but choosing to live as one because we didn't want to live apart. I got that now. I got the intricate parts of how love could be kind and forgiving. How a couple could work past their transgressions and an argument didn't mean a breakup. I wanted it all with Conner. I wanted it forever.

I put every ounce of passion and emotion I had in my body toward every kiss we shared. Neither of us came up for air; we breathed for each other. Hands, sighs, grunts, and nips furiously overtook, and neither of us fought it. We gave in, gladly.

Conner didn't speak or even respond to my apology. He never spilled his guts, telling me how much he loved me or needed me. He did show me though.

Three times.

CHAPTER 13
CONNER

I FOUGHT two more fights before Richard contacted me for a meeting. I figured he'd come calling after meeting him in Las Vegas at Steele's fight, but less than a month after our first introduction was much quicker than I'd expected. The thought of losing my privacy was something I still wasn't sure about, but figured meeting with him wouldn't hurt. Money talked to most people, and I was no exception.

"Are you nervous?" Willow asked, while stirring the contents on her stove.

"Nah. I mean, regardless, I still have a job, right?" I stole a French fry off her plate and dodged her swat at my ass.

"True. But it could be an awesome opportunity. Even Steele says so."

"Yeah, but Steele is used to it. When those people line up outside the gym, he approaches them with no problem. He answers their questions, and takes selfies without complaint. I don't want to talk to people. And I sure as shit don't want to take pictures with them."

She giggled at my gruffness. "Oh, it won't be so bad. And you know, I could do a story on you, then people wouldn't be so interested. They're curious, that's all. When you don't give them anything, that's when they want to know more." She brought our dinner to the table where I had already taken a seat.

"Fuck no. The last thing I want to do is make people feel like they have a right to know me."

"Suit yourself. But don't complain when I'm spending extra time with Gage and Tommy to get the inside track." She winked. "Dana told me today depending on how well my interviews go, there may be a spot with *The Mat* on the line. Can you imagine? One of my articles in pages of *The Mat*?"

Her excitement about her job thrilled me. I'd never been in a position where my emotions mirrored someone else's before. When she was happy, I was happy. When she was upset, I was upset. When she was playful, I was playful. No matter what Willow was feeling, I wanted to feel it too.

"You can do your interviews at my place," I suggested.

She glanced at me over her shoulder and grinned. "Or I could just do them here."

I couldn't remember a time she had looked more beautiful. My stomach twisted and turned, churning almost, from the guilt associated with my fall from the wagon in Las Vegas. There was a piece of me that wanted to just put it out there; admit to relapsing and taking one hundred percent responsibility. But we'd finally just gotten back to normal after the Simone fiasco, not to mention the fact I'd been so angry with her for not believing in me when it turned out—she hadn't been wrong. Bringing up my lie by omission at this point seemed daft. It was over. It happened. I felt like shit for it, and it seemed useless to risk losing her over it. I had my head on straight now. Ruining what we had wasn't a gamble I was willing to take.

"Guess who I've got a date with in an hour?" Gage winked, knowing he was pissing me off.

"Date? I doubt it." I stepped inside the cage, ready for my spar with Steele.

He chuckled, grabbing his bag and walked toward the door. "I'll let you know how it goes."

"That asshole better watch it." Steele laughed, pushing me in the back.

We'd barely gotten started when a newbie walked in. I hadn't noticed at first, but Steele stood straight up, stopping us in our tracks. Following his gaze, I watched cautiously as a tall blonde glanced around the gym, excitement plain on her face.

Steele exited the cage, pulling off his head gear and wiping his face with a towel as he approached her. I waited curiously, wondering what she wanted. There had been a total of two women who'd ever even been inside the facility, as far as I knew, and those were Willow and Lena. Lena of course, never worked out, and Willow had only been there for defense classes.

She followed Steele to his office. Her crop-top fell loosely off her shoulder and her tight pants fit perfectly, sitting low on her hips. Her shoulders were back, and her head lifted high. Her body was lean, and her disposition screamed fearless. She was beautiful, and I knew my buddy wasn't going to be able to resist her, considering he'd basically ended our session for the day just to talk to her.

The last thing Steele needed was a distraction, considering he only had a couple of fights left before entering retirement. I wanted him to go out on top. If anyone deserved it, it was him. He had a meeting in a couple of weeks with his manager and Richard, where they'd hammer out the details and the announcement.

I put my gear away, knowing my work out for the day was over. Leaving the gym, I roamed around town, not ready to go home. The problem was, I'd waged war with myself, time and time again. My dishonesty with Willow had been eating away at me, and I knew she could tell. It didn't help that my dip in the deep end of my disease kept whispering in my ear. Not that I would ever admit it out loud, but I was struggling. I found myself consumed with the need to drink every time I wasn't with her. I hated myself for it. I hated that I didn't feel strong enough when she wasn't around. I couldn't put that weight on her.

While aimlessly wandering around, I once again found my way to the liquor store. Only this time, I parked in the parking lot across the street. I turned my truck off and sat there, staring at the joint like a creepy voyeur. I watched at least twenty people park, go inside, and return to their vehicles with their brown bags in tow. Their stories played out in my mind. Who were they? Did they just want a beer with dinner? Were they fighting the battle of their lives like I was?

I swallowed, feeling lower than ever. Why was I torturing myself? My life was going well. I had a decent job, and I had a woman I loved. She was everything I never knew I could have, supporting me constantly, lifting me up in ways no one before her had been able to.

I smiled, realizing what Willow provided me was enough. I didn't need the drink, nor did I want the numbness I felt when I gave into it. In fact, I wanted to feel what my life was becoming. All I had to do was change my thought pattern, and that would change my attitude.

With a renewed sense of self, I pulled out of the parking lot, empty-handed. Mentally encouraging myself, I gained control of my wayward thoughts. I just needed to concentrate on where I was going, not where I'd been.

Instead of driving home, I decided to go to Willow's. Plus, I wanted to check in on that dickhead, Gage, and make sure he wasn't flirting with my girl.

He's totally flirting with your girl.

Of course, Willow wouldn't take him seriously, but at least my being there would force him to tone it down. Maybe.

Instead of knocking, I let myself in, overhearing them in the kitchen before I saw them. "Honey, I'm home," I called over their laughter. They were laughing, probably at something stupid Gage had said.

"Hey, baby." Willow greeted me with a kiss.

"You about done?"

Gage crossed his arms and grinned. "Just gettin' started."

"We're almost finished," Willow scolded him.

"Good. I'm taking you out tonight."

"Really? Where?"

"It's a surprise." I had only just decided. I realized I'd been so caught up in my own shit, I had never celebrated her new job, or how well she was doing at it. I grimaced, disappointed. I had to do better by her. And I would start tonight.

"Sorry, Gage. My man is taking me somewhere, and I have to get ready. I'll come down to the gym later this week and we'll finish."

"Great. It's another date then." Gage punched me in the shoulder, then quickly ran to the door because he knew I'd punch him back.

Willow laughed. "Why do you hate him? Poor guy. He's harmless." She wrapped her arms around my neck.

"Because he flirts with my girl. He's lucky I don't kick his ass."

While Willow showered, I Googled my way through things to do in Boston. Luckily, the downtown theater had a running show and had tickets available on short notice. They weren't the best seats, but beggars couldn't be choosers. We made a quick pit stop at my house so I could shower and change clothes before we were on our way to a show I didn't exactly want to see, but I knew she would. It was about celebrating her, anyhow. And she'd love it.

"Conner! I've been dying to see this. I can't believe you got us tickets. I was going to come with Lena before the end of the run," she said as we took our seats in the ancient theater.

I smiled at her excitement. "I'm glad. I'm proud of you, babe. You're killing it."

She smiled and kissed my cheek. "Thanks."

"Even though you're interviewing dumbasses, I'm glad you're doing an article on Steele's gym. He deserves the hype."

"He does. You know, if you ever changed your mind . . ." The eagerness behind her eyes was hard for me to turn down. When she looked so happy, I fought myself internally to tell her no.

"I don't want to be in it."

"I get it. Dana did request I ask you, though. She has some sort of fascination with you, I think." She winked.

"Why?" My hackles rose, my defensive instincts climbing higher with each word she spoke. I didn't want or need some freelance editor interested in me.

"I'm not sure. Once she found out we were dating, she's been acting a little strange."

"Strange how?"

"I don't know." She handed me a piece of gum she'd just taken out of her purse. "I thought it was a little odd at first, but then I thought about how she's middle-aged and not married. Maybe she's just enamored with young love?"

"We're not that young." It wasn't like we were crazed teenagers.

"I don't know. She just asks about you a lot." I scowled. "Not like *that*. She thinks the article would be better if you were in it, because you're on the cusp of going pro, and your name would draw more readers."

I was skeptical, but wouldn't push the issue. Our night out was supposed to be about celebrating her job, not knocking it. I kept a mental note about her boss's curiosity, however. I couldn't imagine why a lady who wrote and edited stories on the top three items to keep in a woman's purse would be so interested in a no-name fighter who may or may not go pro. I didn't like it. And I especially didn't like her pushing my girlfriend to dig up a story on me.

The play was boring as hell. I fell asleep twice. Willow kept elbowing me every time I lost interest and from the chill inside the cab of my truck on the way home, she wasn't pleased. It wasn't like I could help it though. I hated frilly shit like musicals, but the point was I'd taken her. I had made the effort.

Unable to accept her being angry with me, I pulled her onto my lap, not giving her the chance to exit my truck once I pulled into her driveway. "Forgive me?"

"I don't have much choice, do I?" she said breathlessly, as I kissed the side of her neck.

My hands roamed up her thighs as I pushed her dress up around her waist. My palms were big enough that they covered the tops of her legs. I brushed my thumbs on the inside of her panties, barely caressing the smooth skin I found there. Her breath hitched. As did mine. Her warmth engulfed me, mimicking a heated volcano on the verge of eruption inside my body.

As my fingertips found the inside of her folds, my lips found hers. Slick. Hot. Lazy. It was too much and not enough at the same time. Willow's sighs and barely-there gasps were enough to create a warm tingling on the inside. It was as if my blood boiled—from pure ecstasy. Sucking on her tongue, I tilted my index finger, attempting to reach the special part of her center designated only for me. Three caresses, two pulls on her tongue, and one firm grasp of her ass cheek with my other hand, was all it took for my woman to soar. I greedily continued lazy strokes inside her panties, reveling in the feel of her release on my fingers.

I smiled behind our kiss as she went completely limp in my arms. Nothing would ever beat the natural beauty of a sated Willow. There wasn't a natural waterfall, a mountain, or a skyline in the world that could give me the joy she gave me when she fell apart in my arms.

"I really hate you sometimes."

"I just spent two and half hours at a fucking play. I think if anyone hates anyone, it's me that hates you, sweetheart." I pulled my hand from her panties and squeezed her thighs.

"After what you just did, you can hate me anytime you want." Her voice was dreamlike.

I snickered and proceeded to help her out of my truck. I walked her to the door, hating that I had to go home. I had shit to do, and a conference call in the morning with a committee from the AFL. I still wasn't sure if I was going to sign, but Steele told me that they'd start me off with a light contract. That had settled my nerves a little.

Eight hours later, I paced my living room for twenty full minutes, waiting on the call. I hadn't told Willow about it. I didn't want to get her hopes up, in case they decided not to offer me anything.

My phone buzzed in my front pocket. I answered after the second ring. "Hello?"

"Conner Payne?"

"Yes."

"Hey, man. This is Stuart Mitchell. I have Richard and Tom, the league's lawyer, here with me."

"How's it going? Richard, Tom, nice to speak with you." I hated formalities. I wasn't any good at them.

"Very well, thank you. I've been talking to Steele about you for a while now. Your tapes are incredible. I like your tenacity. It's like a breath of fresh air," Richard said.

"Thanks."

"I'd like to see you fight in person before I make an official offer. But given that things go well, I'd be willing to offer you a two-match contract. They would probably be within four months of each other. If you win, you'll receive a bonus for each match. If you're happy with the terms of agreement, we'll go from there."

I didn't give myself time to think about it. I was afraid I'd back out if I did. So, I agreed, ending the phone call. The opportunity could be awesome for my career. It could also be devastating for my personal life. The kicker was, I didn't know if one was worth risking the other. As many years as I'd waited for freedom, I finally had a somewhat decent shot at it, and I didn't know how I felt about it.

CHAPTER 14
WILLOW

SINCE THE NEWS had gotten out that Conner signed a two-fight deal with the AFL, things were beginning to take off for him. Local fans were waiting outside Steele's gym, expecting pictures and autographs. He wasn't handling it well. I talked to Steele about it, wondering what we could do to help him. Conner hadn't opened up about why he was so stressed about it, but deep down, I felt like I knew where the anxiety was coming from. He was worried someone would expose his crippling past.

Dana was constantly on my case at work. Our relationship had gone from pleasant to annoying. In a matter of months, her personality had done a one-eighty. At first, I'd chalked it up to nothing personal. Maybe she'd gone through a break-up. Possibly her pet could have died. But she was showing no signs of mercy in recent months, and kept pressuring me to make Conner's gains in the professional world public. I grew suspicious of her curiosity in my boyfriend. Her emails were becoming not only rude, but downright threatening.

She claimed in the last email, she was having trouble finding work for me outside of the sports world. I knew that was a lie because there had been no trouble beforehand. In fact, I'd been paid more in the last four months free-lancing than I had in the last year at my old job. With two advances, and a steady weekly salary, I was doing better than ever before. And more than half that salary came from magazines that had nothing to do with sports.

After Conner patiently listened to me complain about my boss, and how she'd basically threatened me with no work, he stepped up. Hugging me tight, he agreed to an interview, as long as I left his personal life out of it. I told him again and again that I would figure something out, but he insisted—claimed he didn't like to see me stressed.

As much as I loved him for his sacrifice, I would never ask him to do something he wasn't comfortable with. He told me he trusted me, and that he knew people were going to write about him at some point. He would rather it be me, than anyone else. I took pride in that.

I walked into the gym, ready to surprise him with lunch, when I noticed most of the guys in a huddle in the middle of the weight area. They were watching something on one of their cell phones. I didn't want to interrupt, so I kept quiet while walking up on them.

"This is no place for a girl. I won't tell you again," a gruff voice said. The sound on the video wasn't all that great.

"But I want to be more than a secretary for this business. I've wanted more for a long time."

The older man chuckled, like the girl in the video's claim was absurd. "No. There's a job waiting for you in the front office."

"Why won't you take me seriously? I've worked my ass off for an opportunity. I know I can do it."

"You have no idea what it takes to make it in this business. I've done my best to shelter you from it. Girls have no business near a cage. It's a man's sport. Always has been, always will be—as long as I own it. Now get your ass down to the front office, or don't. Either way, you're not breaking a nail on my watch."

My eyes were glued to the screen, the same as all the guys in the circle. Gage held his phone out so that everyone could see the man display one of the oldest forms of sexism. He'd straight up told the girl it was an all-boys club. I felt sorry for her. The video cut off abruptly. The quality was poor, and it seemed like someone had videoed it conspicuously.

"What a dick, man. There are girls all over who can fight or what-ever she wants to do." Gage shook his head.

Steele looked disgusted. "I've known Richard for a long time. That surprises me. He's always been fair with his contracts. I would have never pictured him treating his own daughter like that."

"That was his daughter?" I asked.

The guys looked up in surprise, not having realized I was there yet. Conner hugged me. "What are you doing here?"

I held up the bag with his favorite deli sandwich in tow. "I brought you lunch."

"Thanks, babe."

"So, why is her dad telling her what she can and can't do? I mean, she looked grown to me." It was none of my business, but what a dick! It was bad enough for women to be treated less than equal by society, but by your own father? I couldn't imagine.

"He keeps her out of the business. I've only seen her a couple of times. She mostly stays out of the public eye," Gage said.

"There's not a woman's league? Where she could shine in her own right?" I'd never heard of one, but then again, I'd only been introduced to the fighting world recently.

"Not pro," Steele replied.

"That doesn't seem fair."

"Life ain't fair, baby girl." Gage shrugged.

I could tell the guys weren't going to jump on my feminist band-wagon. They agreed that there was sexism being displayed, but doing something about it was a different story. It seemed that was the way the world worked. Most people didn't want to solve a problem that didn't have anything to do with them.

"Are you nervous?" I asked Conner as we walked over to a bench in the corner. I unloaded the food from the bag.

"Nah."

"It's kind of a big deal. I mean, it's in New York!" I couldn't help my excitement. Ever since he'd told me his first official match would be in NYC, I'd been counting down the days. I wasn't nervous about the fight—I had all the faith in the world in his abilities—but I couldn't help but be concerned about what it meant for him personally.

"Doesn't matter to me where I fight. I'm just ready to handle business and collect the pay check."

I rolled my eyes. Of course, he wasn't concerned with Canal street, but I was. I'd started saving a couple of weeks ago. I meant to shop until I dropped, whether he was game or not. Lena was traveling with me, so either way, I planned on having fun, *after* my man won his fight.

"Lena got approved for her days off, so she will fly out with us."

"Cool." He finished his sandwich. "Thanks for bringing me lunch. I better get back to work."

"Okay. Don't forget we have a date tonight."

"We do?" He looked genuinely confused.

"The interview?"

"Oh." His face fell.

I brushed a piece of hair off his forehead. "It will be painless. I promise we'll stick to facts."

"I trust you. I just stress about shit being out there." He glanced around, even though the guys had long since left us alone.

"I know, babe. I promise everything will stay professional, and I'll show you the article before I submit it."

"All right." He kissed me and walked me to my car.

I had known for a while how paranoid Conner would be about people being curious about him, but I couldn't be sure that was what was bugging him now. He'd been acting strange since Steele's last fight in Vegas, and he still wasn't back to normal. At first, I'd chalked it up to it being our first fight. I mean, there were a couple of days there, where neither one of us knew if we were going to be okay, but enough time had passed now.

As the time passed, I was beginning to think it was a little bit of everything. He was going through so many changes. Our relationship was a first for him, in a long time. He also had to adjust to life outside of prison, deal with the reason he was in prison, and now he was about to turn pro in a profession he never even knew he wanted. Those scenarios would be overwhelming for anyone. And it seemed to be bothering him more than he was willing to admit. The only thing I could do was be there for him, and try to keep our personal lives as normal as possible.

With knowing my man so well, I mistakenly assumed our interview would be a piece of cake. Turned out, it was harder than I'd expected. Every time I asked a question, he answered with, "I don't know." As in, he didn't want to answer anything other than his height and weight. I finally got him to relent on his initial meeting with Steele. We took the interview that route; how he trained with Steele. I vaguely mentioned the local fights, but concentrated more on his future.

To date, his interview had been the shortest I'd ever submitted, but I figured since I was submitting three other stories, maybe we'd still get the spot in the sports magazine I normally wrote for.

Two days later, I met with Dana at the local coffee shop for her approval on the stories. She insisted on meeting in person, stating the article on the athletes was more important because it would go national. I wasn't sure how well our meeting would go, considering the last email we exchanged was somewhat hostile. I'd taken it personally when she'd said I could either get on board with her vision, or get off at the next port.

She was all business as she pulled her thick rimmed glasses out of her purse. "I want to see your interview with Conner Payne."

"Okay. I have Gage, Steele—"

"Payne's please." She held out her hand, ready for me to hand it over.

I planned on telling her that the other guys' interviews were pretty damn good, if I did say so myself, but she wasn't interested. Gage's was hilarious. Steele's was inspirational. Conner's was . . . basic. Not by any fault in my writing abilities, but because I would do everything in my power to protect him and his feelings.

I handed the folder over and waited for her response. Her eyes focused on the black print, reading each word ferociously. She seemed hungry for his story. I fought the urge to rip the papers from her hands. Why was she so interested in him? He was obviously the most important person on *my* priority list, but for the readers? Or for Dana, who was an editor? I assumed the playboy, or the pro-fighter would have piqued more interest.

I pulled the other folders out of my bag and waited for her to finish.

She turned the page and frowned. "What the hell is this?" She looked up at me over the top of her glasses.

"What's what?" I wasn't sure where she was going.

"There's nothing substantial here. Nothing about his personal life. Nothing about you, his girlfriend, or his past. Where is he from? Does he have any siblings?" She released the paper, but continued talking. My eyes darted to the stapled paper as it fell flat on the table. "What did he do before he became a fighter? Where did he work?"

I swallowed, considering my next words. Her demanding tone took me by surprise, and pissed me off at the same time. "Conner is a private person. And the reason there's nothing about me in there is because the article isn't about me. It's about making it in a profession most people don't know about. I have nothing to do with that world."

"Are you fucking kidding me? You can't be that dense, Willow. The readers don't give a shit about Conner striking up a friendship with a fighter who's about to retire. They don't care about his record. They care about where he's been, and who he's been with, which is you."

"I disagree. But either way, I think if you'll read the other interviews, you'll see that we have all of that. These are well-rounded. There's something here for everyone." I wasn't about to let her intimidate me.

She crossed her arms. "We're at an impasse then."

"I'm not changing it." I mirrored her disposition, crossing my own arms. I didn't want to lose my job, but Conner was off limits. At least where she was concerned.

She leaned back in her chair, either sizing me up, or thinking about what to say next. I couldn't tell. Everything in my body quivered, waiting. I'd been able to put away a good chunk of my last four checks because they were more than I needed to live off of, but I was nowhere near wealthy. Plus, dammit, some of that money was for New York. Conner had already covered our flights and hotel rooms, but I had my own plans, and I would never ask him to support my shopping habit.

"I'll run it, but I'm doing it on a trial basis. If this doesn't go over well, and the magazine isn't happy with it, I'm afraid we'll be cutting ties. They are one of my biggest clients, and I have others who write for them. I can't risk losing them."

"I understand." I handed over the last of my paperwork and gathered my belongings.

I was livid. There was no way I was sitting there for another minute, while she threatened me with my job. We said our goodbyes, and I drove home.

The drive did me no good. I felt like I'd been deflated. Best case—the magazine would sell a shit-ton of copies once they hit the stands. Worst case—I had to start over... again.

Wiping my eyes, I plastered a smile on my face before I pulled into Conner's driveway. He had enough on his plate, without adding my work woes to it. Plus, he was worried more than I'd ever seen him about the interview going live. The last thing I wanted to do was tell him how Dana basically called it shit. I'd just have to be patient and supportive, while I waited to see if I would be employed the following week or not.

Luckily, New York happened before I received any news. I needed the distraction.

The hotel was only a few minutes from the airport, which I was thankful for. I wanted to freshen up. There was something about flying that always made me feel dirty. Like being in an enclosed space for that long gave me other peoples' cooties.

I'd made dinner reservations for us prior to arriving. At least I could be certain one of our nights in New York would be relaxed. The others would depend on how Conner's fight went.

"You look beautiful, baby."

I smiled from Conner's sweet compliment. "Thank you. Ready?"

"One sec," he said as he stood from the chair.

He was so handsome. Dressed in black pants and a black button down, I could see his muscular build flexing through the material. Walking toward me, he grinned, which made me smile.

Grabbing my waist, he pulled me into him. His lips reached mine, softly at first. Then, greedily. My body buzzed with anticipation. My mind lulled to a sacred place, where the only thing I could think about was the way Conner loved me. How he showed me instead of told me.

"I messed your lipstick up."

Playfully, I pushed him away. "Quit bragging."

"Never. It's kind of the only thing I care about."

Taking a quick look in the mirror, I laughed. "Liar. You care about me."

From behind, Conner wrapped his arms around my waist and placed his chin on my shoulder. "More than you'll ever know, Wil."

"Let's go eat, boyfriend. Then—"

Conner grabbed my hand, and all but dragged me to the door. We both laughed and I couldn't help but sigh. I loved the sound of a happy Conner.

Steele and Lena joined us at the restaurant after we were seated. For some reason, they chose to get their own cab. I briefly wondered whether they would end up dating or not, but each time we were all out together, he always went home with someone else. And Lena didn't seem to mind. She'd never once talked about him any other way than platonic. Of course, she agreed with me that he was a catch, but they always joked with each other. There was never a seriousness to them.

"You ready, dude?" Steele asked.

"Sure."

"How are you guys so nonchalant about your fights?" Lena grabbed a roll and pinched off a piece. "I'd be shitting my pants leading up to it."

"We spend ten hours a day training for them," Steele said. "It's like second nature when we get out there."

"I, for one, am ready for it to be over." I squeezed Conner's thigh under the table. It wasn't that I didn't have confidence in him, but watching someone try to hurt him wasn't high on my priority list.

Understanding, he brought my hand to his mouth and placed a soft kiss on my palm. "It'll be over soon enough."

"Want to split a bottle of wine?" Lena asked peering at me over her menu.

My stomach lurched at the thought. Conner nodded, telling me he was fine with me drinking. "I'm good," I politely declined, and leaned into him.

"Bruce called me today. Told me that Richard would be here tomorrow," Steele said to Conner.

"Cool," Conner replied.

"Is he at all the fights?" I asked, still unsure of how the pro league worked.

"Pretty much. And his son is usually around. I can't stand that little pecker-head." Steele grimaced.

"Why?" I asked.

"For one, he's an asshole. And two," Steele held up two fingers, "he's a silver-spooned pussy."

"That's harsh." Lena chuckled. "Not a thing in the world wrong with a silver spoon, but what makes him such a pussy?" she asked, after she thanked the waitress for her wine.

"That kid has never fought a day in his life, yet he has opinions on how to win them." Steele shook his head. "He's condescending. No one likes him."

"How old is he?" I asked.

"Not sure." He lifted a shoulder. "Twenty-five, maybe?"

"His sister, Navie, doesn't seem like that," I added. "Not that I know her or anything, but after I saw that horrible video, I googled her. There were a few interviews she did with her family, and I also saw she graduated from Yale. She seems really smart and kind."

"We've crossed paths, but I don't remember formally meeting her. She's hot as hell though," Steele grinned, mischievously.

"Right . . . because that's most important." Lena laughed.

Steele winked in Lena's direction. "Hotness is always important. If you ain't pretty, we can't hang."

Lena rolled her eyes. "I was just about to ask how you weren't married yet, but never mind." Steele tensed a little, and released a nervous chuckle.

I studied him, but he continued eating his dinner, leaving me to wonder if his initial reaction to Lena's response actually meant anything.

After dinner, Conner and I returned to our hotel room. I was too antsy to enjoy a distraction and I honestly didn't think it in Conner's best interest to have one. Other than me. Climbing into bed, I snuggled up to Conner's back. His smell was intoxicating. It was like a flood of endorphins released in my body every time I got close enough to truly feel him. We lay in silence, knowing the world was continuing along at its normal pace on the bustling New York City streets; but in our bubble, there was peace. Until I spoke my strange thoughts aloud.

"What was prison like?" The question was muffled, as my lips were pressed firmly into his back.

For a split second, I regretted bringing it up. The night before his big fight was probably not the best time to dig up old, painful memories.

The muscles in his back tensed, making me clench him tighter. My cheek rubbed the same spot trying to help him relax. It killed me on the inside that I needed to know. I never wanted him to remember a time in his life that wasn't happy, but for our sake . . . I needed to know what he went through.

"You wouldn't like it." His voice was thick, but his tone was light.

I opened my mouth, scraping his skin with my teeth. Relief flowed out of my body like a wave at his joke.

He turned toward me, pulling my body into his. I snuggled close, waiting for him to continue. "It was crowded." His brow furrowed. "Mostly, it was just routine, like the same thing every single day."

"Is it anything like the movies portray?" I asked, after I saw he was okay discussing it. "Did you have to watch your back constantly?"

"Yeah, baby." He hugged me close, taking comfort from my body. I thought he'd drifted off; he was so still. But after a few moments, he rubbed my hair softly, and kissed the top of my head. "I mostly stayed to myself. There's a lot of drama there. At first, I counted the days, but eventually, I just did what I could to stay busy."

"I'm so sorry you had to go through that. Sometimes, when I think about it, it makes me want to cry."

"Don't." He lifted my chin so that I could see his eyes. "I mean it. Don't cry for me. We're here now, and that's all that matters."

"Okay." I smiled at his positivity. "Hate you."

"I hate you too. Now go to sleep. I've got some ass to kick tomorrow, so we can get back home and back to normal. I hate this fucking city."

I chuckled and kissed his lips. "Good night, hater."

CHAPTER 15
CONNER

"YOU GOT THIS, MAN," Steele said in my ear. "Stay focused, and as soon as you get your shot, take his ass to the ground."

"Got it." I put my mouthpiece in and entered the cage.

My gaze remained trained on my opponent, even though mentally, I was struggling to focus. I could see the poster boards, and hands waving from all directions. I didn't like it. It made me uneasy with all their eyes on me. Chaos ensued in my gut, swirling around and around, until a pang of nausea hit me. I swallowed back the bile, and popped up on the balls of my feet to stretch my calves.

Scott Miller stood in his corner, eyeing me. I gave him one nod, and that was it. It was all he was getting; it was all the crowd was getting. I came here to do a job. I took a deep breath as I took the center of the cage. It was go time.

"Get him low!" Steele called from my corner.

I will if I can.

The son-of-a-bitch was tougher than he looked. He was wiry, and hard as fuck to pin down. I tried two takedowns, and he got out of both of them. Before I could recover my footing, I took a blow to the ribs. Air gushed out of my lungs, making me squint in pain. Endorphins released, and my muscles relaxed after contracting from the blows. Nothing compared to the rush, except maybe alcohol, but that wasn't an option anymore. Not since I had Willow.

Just like every other time I was in the cage, I smiled, eager for the chase. Something came alive in me the moment I realized I was going to have to work harder for the win. Adrenaline shot through my veins with every punch he threw. I took three more before I began throwing my own.

I pushed him back, ready to tear into him, when they called the round. I strolled back to the corner, keeping my composure, even though I was so amped up, I wanted to sprint.

"Don't let him get too many in. You'll use all your energy defending," Steele coached from the corner.

"Got it." I wasn't going to let the fucker hit me again. The fight had already gone one round too many for my taste.

Taking my stance in the center of the cage, I glanced over at Willow, which was a mistake. Her eyes were gleaming, her hands folded tightly at her lips. She was worried. I didn't like seeing her like that, especially when there was nothing to be concerned about.

A pang of guilt set low in my belly. It had actually been a fun five minutes for me, and she'd been tense the entire time, probably biting her lips to the point she'd ripped skin. Either that, or her horrible habit of biting her nails had returned after a decent three week run.

Round two began, and I threw two punches to Miller's gut, followed by an Axe kick. His step faltered and that was all the opening I needed. Pouncing on him like he was my prey, I folded him into the position I needed him in, so that I could apply an arm bar. Three squeezes, then a tap. I released my hold, rolled to my feet, and walked back to my corner.

"Payne! Payne! Payne!" Kids were screaming. Dudes were high-fiving. Women were jumping up and down in their barely-there tops. Steele was grinning from ear to ear, and all I could think about was getting to Willow. Comforting her and showing her I was more than okay.

The ref took forever to check on Miller. I walked to the center, annoyed I had to wait for them to announce the winner. What I hadn't factored in was the announcer making a spectacle of it. This was no longer the little cage I'd been used to fighting in. No, this was the pro circuit, and they were damn sure going to live it up for the paying fans.

"One down . . ." Steele slapped a hand on my shoulder when I made it to the side of the cage.

"One to go," I finished, and immediately began searching for Willow in the crowd. Steele and the other members of my crew were trying to push me down the tunnel to the locker room, but I needed to set eyes on her first.

I sidestepped well-wishers, and grown men whooping and hollering as I passed, frantic to find her. I turned a trashcan over, dumping out the contents in the process, and stood on it, thinking if I could just get higher, I'd be able to spot her from the ground. It took everything I had in me not to get on the PA system and demand people to shut the fuck up. They continued to congratulate me over and over, not even bothering to notice I was in the middle of a mini mental breakdown.

I got separated from Steele while searching for Willow. That's when I realized she may have already made her way to the tunnel. I started that way, ignoring the congratulatory slaps on my back.

"Willow back here?" I asked, walking through the doorway of the locker room.

"Haven't seen her." Steele's eyes grew darker once he took in my worried expression. "Did she say she'd meet you here?"

"No."

I'm stupid and didn't lay down concrete plans, not expecting the crowd to rush the cage after my win.

"Okay, man. She's probably just waiting out the crowd. It was packed out there."

Dread filled my gut. Something didn't feel right. I knew something was wrong.

"No, she isn't. I know she isn't."

Sweat filled my pores. I felt sick. I'd kill someone if she was injured. I swore I'd never go back on the inside, but I never had anything worth risking it for. Now, I did.

"Call her."

Taking his advice, I clicked on her name. "She's not answering," I told him after the third ring. Closing my eyes, I racked my brain for any explanation that made sense. "There's no way in hell she would have just left." Running my still-wrapped hands through my hair, I cursed.

"Don't—"

I stepped up to him nose to nose. "Don't tell me not to worry." I was holding my shit together by a thread. My chest rose and fell in what falsely conveyed as calm breaths. I wasn't calm. I was freaking the fuck out on the inside, and aside from knowing that I had to find her, I couldn't form a coherent thought about anything else.

That's when Lena walked in. She glanced from me to Steele, confused. "Where's Willow?"

My fears were becoming realized. "Wasn't she with you?"

"No, we got separated, and—"

I threw my bag on the ground, grabbed my phone, and ran toward the exit.

"Conner!" Steele tried to grab my arm, but I pulled away from him and blew past Lena. "I'll stay here and look, man. We'll find her!" I continued further away from him, and he kept calling for me. "Let's make a plan. Conner!"

I didn't respond, my mind already inventing devastating scenarios of her being hurt. I went out behind the building and searched every crevice. Then I walked through four different alleyways, trying to think of the darkest spots imaginable. I stepped over two homeless people and a small dog, searching behind a dumpster. For a split second, my mind went back to Vegas, when I'd taken the whiskey from the poor old man on the street. I bent over, my head all but dangling, forcing the bile trekking up the back of my throat back down. I spit and stood to my full height.

Glancing around, I felt out of control. I was in an alley, looking for my girlfriend—who I wasn't sure had just taken an alternate route to the tunnel and was waiting on me inside the locker room.

My fears from my past were taking over. I'd overreacted, scared out of my mind that maybe Mikey had shown up after hearing about my fight, and done something horrific to her because of me. His popping up in my life after two years had me convinced he had something up his sleeve. Steele probably thought I was nuts. I should have told him who Mikey was the night my nemesis from the penitentiary decided to track me down. If, for no other reason, he could have helped me keep an eye on him.

My phone vibrated in my pocket. "Yeah?" I answered Steele's call, praying he had Willow with him.

"She's okay."

"Where is she?" Heat scorched my neck, and fire ignited in my chest; the flames bellowing toward the sky.

"She's just shaken up—"

"Where the fuck is she?"

I couldn't make out the muffled voices in the background. "We're in the locker room."

I hung up before he could give me any more information. I ran five blocks without stopping. I hadn't prayed—*really* prayed—in years, yet in that moment, before I opened the large metal door, I prayed Willow had no physical injuries. I wasn't sure I was strong enough to deal with it all if someone had touched her.

The tension in the room was thick. Steele sat facing Willow, who was seated in the corner chair, her legs tucked underneath her, making her seem like a small child. She looked fragile and exhausted. Lena was seated next to Steele, unmistakably shaken up.

Willow glanced up when I knelt next to her.

I took her in my arms, thankful she was with me. "What happened?"

CHAPTER 16
WILLOW

I'D NEVER FORGET the fear in Conner's eyes, silently pleading for me to tell him I was all right. I glanced over at Steele, who stood with his thick arms crossed, pity etched deep in his expression. Lena stood next to him, both her arms folded around her middle, her demeanor rigid but relieved.

"I needed to use the restroom halfway through the fight, but held off because I didn't want to miss any of it. After you won, I went, knowing I'd have enough time before meeting you here." I shivered at the memory.

Conner stroked my hair, urging me to go on.

"I didn't think to check the toilet paper roll before I locked myself in the stall. There were other women in there, so I didn't think anything about asking the person next to me to hand me a couple of squares under the stall." I swallowed thickly.

"But when the person next to me handed me the toilet paper, I could see that it was a man's hand. I took it from him, confused at first, but then—everything was eerily quite. The voices I'd heard moments before were no more. It scared me, knowing I was alone in the restroom with a strange man."

"Fuck!" Conner swore. Agony filled his face, and Steele moved toward us.

"I'm okay. He didn't hurt me. But Navie . . ." I winced, knowing she was hurt. "I didn't get the chance to make sure she was okay, because Lena and Steele burst through the door just as she was going hands-on with him."

"Who? Who's *he*?" I asked.

"It was the same guy who cornered you in Vegas," Steele spoke up.

Conner put his forehead on my hand that was clutching the arm of the chair. Confusion set in as I realized what Steele had said.

"What guy?" I asked Conner.

"We need a minute," Conner said to Steele and Lena.

"Man, we still have to give a statement to the police. They're with Navie now, in the next room." Steele didn't budge.

"We need a minute," Conner repeated, pinning Steele with a look so dark, a whole new concern grew deep inside in my gut.

Steele nodded, then eyed Lena. "We'll be outside."

Conner stood beside me, the silence stretching out so far, I wondered if he was ever going to explain. Then he growled and hung his head. "His name is Mikey Godwin. We served time in the same prison. We never got along. He found me in Vegas, the night—"

"The night of Steele's fight?"

"Yeah." He sighed. "Did he touch you?"

"He—frightened me," I admitted.

"Did he *touch* you?"

"No. Navie walked in and—Conner, she got hurt." I wiped a tear from my eye and sniffed. Lord, I felt so bad. That girl had saved me, and got hurt in the process.

"Tell me, baby. Tell me everything."

"After I took the toilet paper from him, I pulled my pants up and tried to think of what to do next. I grabbed my phone out of my purse and sent a text to Lena, telling her where I was. I should have just waited to go to the bathroom."

He grabbed my face. "Don't you dare do that. Don't blame yourself for this."

I shook off the inner turmoil and continued. "I stayed in the stall, waiting, but he ripped it the door open. He broke the lock."

Tears pooled in Conner's eyes. I took a deep breath and finished telling him the horrific chain of events. "He told me payback was a bitch."

"Baby." Conner let out a sob and pulled me into his arms. I held on just as tight, both of us breathing the best we could through our tears. I was still shaking when I pulled back.

"Navie walked in when he had me backed up into the corner. She questioned him, and I yelled for help. Before either of us could escape, Navie punched him. He grabbed her by the hair and threw across the room. Her back landed against the sink. She lunged back at him, punching, kicking, anything she could do. He hit her twice, Conner. She was bleeding."

Conner stood abruptly. Pacing back and forth, his hands kept flexing into clenched fists. He looked ready to tear the roof off the place. I called his name twice, but he didn't answer me. I stood and walked over to him.

"Conner?" I pulled his face down to mine so that we were eye level.

"I'm going to kill him."

I shook my head. "You can't do that."

"The fuck you say? I'm going to fucking murder him."

"Listen to me. The police have him. They caught him. They are talking with Navie now, and—"

Before I could finish, two detectives walked in, followed by Steele and Lena. Conner walked over to the last roll of lockers—as far as he could get from me. Still, I could physically *feel* the reverberations of anger rolling off him.

One of the officers recorded my statement, while the other took notes. I told them everything I knew, including what Conner had just revealed about knowing the guy from prison. Conner paced the length of the locker room during the entire retelling of my story.

Lena sat shocked on the arm of the chair I was sitting in. Every time I mentioned Conner, or his past, she tensed up. I hated that my best friend was learning everything all at once. I would have felt guilty, had I not been so shaken up.

Steele stood quietly in the corner, listening to me, but kept his focus solely on Conner; making sure he was okay, I imagined.

Twenty minutes later, the detectives made their exit. Lena

hugged me, hanging on for dear life. Conner and Steele whispered fervently in the corner, back and forth, until Steele cupped his shoulder, willing him to calm down. Whatever he'd said didn't work.

Conner made a beeline toward me. "Let's go." He grabbed my shoes from the floor and began putting them on my feet.

It was as if he couldn't stand to hear another word about what had transpired. I tugged his arm when we passed the next room on our way out. I couldn't leave without seeing Navie. Walking inside, we found her sitting on a gurney in nothing but her pants and a bra, getting her ribs taped by one of the trainers. She winced as the guy wrapping her pulled the tape tight.

I gasped at the sight of her. "Navie," My voice broke.

"How are you?" she asked.

"Don't worry about me. Are you okay? I'm so sorry."

"I'm fine, Willow. I'm just glad he got caught."

"Me too." I didn't dare tell her Conner knew the man who'd hurt her.

Conner closed the gap between us, leading me the whole way by the hand. "Thank you. Thank you so much. I can never repay you for helping Willow."

"It was nothing. I was at the right place at the right time."

"If you ever need *anything*, you come to me. You saved my life tonight." Conner held out his hand for her to shake.

Navie looked from Conner to me, her eyes softening as she realized how much I meant to him. She shook his hand and nodded. "I appreciate that."

The trainer left her side and she pulled her blouse back over her head. I approached her, wanting to hug her, but at the same time, not wanting to hurt her more. "Thank you."

She pulled me in, patting me on the back. "You're welcome. I'm glad you're okay."

Conner and I left, hand in hand. He didn't loosen his grip on me until we got back to the hotel. I shot Lena and Steele a text, letting them know we'd made it back safely.

I'd thought a little on what I needed to say to him on the way back.

I still wasn't sure as he closed our hotel room, locking it for good measure.

What I did know, was there seemed to be more to his story. I needed to know what that was.

"I don't want any secrets between us."

Conner took my purse from my shoulder and placed it on the side table.

I wanted him to understand what I was saying. I needed him to get that after what had just happened, I was scared. That man, Mikey Godwin, had terrified me, and the only reason he'd targeted me was because of Conner. I wanted to know why. I deserved to know.

"I told you. I know him from prison."

"But why did he try to hurt me? And why didn't you tell me you had a run in with him in Las Vegas?"

Anyone else may not have noticed the small flinch in his shoulders at the mention of Vegas, but I had. My insides turned, knowing for certain in that very moment, he hadn't told me everything.

"I didn't want to worry you with it."

"So, you just figured you'd ignore it and it would go away?" I asked, sitting on the end of the bed.

He sighed and hung his head. "After Simone found me," he averted his eyes, knowing that memory still stung, "she told me that a guy was asking about me. When I found out it was Mikey, I was stunned. I've not had contact with one person from prison since my release." He knelt in front of me. "I confronted him, wondering why he'd tracked me down. I still don't know."

"Go on," I urged.

"When he wouldn't tell me what he was doing there, I got pissed and left. That's when I called you." Something flickered in his eyes. Regret? Pain?

It was like a train wreck. I had to know. Feeling like my heart was bursting at the seams, clawing to get out of my chest. "Is there anything else?"

He grabbed my hands, rubbing them over and over, as if he were trying to keep warm. My feet tingled, setting off alarm signals all throughout my body. I remained silent as my palms began to perspire.

"I can't," he uttered. Shame spread across his face as he looked up at me, taking his concentration off our entwined hands.

"I won't assume. I promised you that much, and I aim to keep it. But you promised some things yourself. Don't be a coward, Conner. Don't lie to me." I expected the truth, and he would have to say it out loud. I wouldn't say the words for him.

"You already know." He pulled away from me and stood. "Just make your decision."

"Not until you admit it." I seethed. Not only from his weakness, but the fact that he'd lied to me for so long about it. We were nothing without trust. My heart broke, hanging on every word he wasn't saying. The emotional distance between us outweighing the physical by miles.

I stood, matching his stance. Working up the courage, I knew what I had to do. If I didn't do in the moment, I'd never do it, and our lives together would never know peace. "We're done. I can't and won't carry your burden."

He spun on a dime, eyes wide with fear. "I haven't asked you to."

"No, you've forced me to, because you keep it secret. I love you enough to help you in any way I can. You should know that. But lying to me and continuing on your path of self-destruction? No. I won't be a part of that. Been there and done that. I care more about myself than that." I snatched my purse off the table and walk to the door.

"Wait! God, please wait," he begged.

I stopped, and stood with my back to him. I closed my eyes, not knowing up from down. I let the silence speak for itself. I waited, wordlessly letting him know I'd at least listen to what he had to say.

"I did," he finally confessed. "I got wasted in Vegas. After I called you back and you accused me of drinking, I lost it. I'd just dealt with the Simone shit. Not two minutes after that, I was confronted by Mikey, and my mind raced with reasons he was seeking me out. I knew none of them were good. But most of all, I couldn't believe that after all we'd been through, after the way I'd opened up to you, you didn't think more of me. You just assumed I turned to the bottle the moment I wasn't with you."

I turned to look at him. "And I was right."

"Not when you first assumed it, you weren't. I hadn't had a drop up until that point. I thought we were beyond shit like that. I have never—ever—accused you of using. Even though I know about your past, I've never accused you of going back there. But you did. It hurt me that you didn't think better of me."

Tears strolled down his cheeks. I tried not to follow his lead, but it was no use. Seeing him so real and raw, it broke me.

"It killed me when you didn't trust me. I got pissed and made a mistake. I swear, Willow. It will never happen again. Never. I'll die before I take another drink."

"I can't—" I tried to speak through my tears. My emotions were all over the place. Breathing and walking at the same time seemed impossible at that moment.

He was in front of me within seconds. "Listen to me!" His large hands cupped my shoulders. "I swear on my life. I can't lose you. You are all that I have."

"Conner, this is too much."

"I need to know that you're not giving up on us." His face contorted, leaving the agony clear for me to see. "I need to know that I still have something to fight for."

"I just need some time. I'm exhausted. I can't deal with all this right now." I sniffed, feeling like a ship lost at sea.

"Look at me." His hands cradled my face, forcing my eyes to his. "I love you, so damn much. And I promise you, it will never happen again. None of this. The drinking, Simone, a criminal from my past, lies, none of it."

God, the depth of my feelings for him scared me, and for the life of me, I couldn't fight them. The uncertainty terrified me. The chance of him hurting me, of me feeling helpless once again, plagued me. But one look at him and I knew I'd forgive him.

It was then I first noticed the cut above his eye. It had stopped bleeding, but a harsh purple bruise was already forming. His lip was busted at the corner, and there was no telling what the rest of his body looked like.

I'd never seen or heard him be so adamant about something. I felt as if I were stepping off a cliff without a harness. It was the first time since my own incident, I'd been faced with a relapse, and I didn't know what to do next.

I stood motionless as he cradled my face, willing me to forgive him for a mistake he'd made. I realized that maybe my words earlier weren't correct. Maybe the whole point of loving an addict wasn't carrying their burden. Maybe it was holding them up, pushing with all your might against their backs, while they carried their own burden. Maybe, all he needed from me was a little support.

"Okay." I nodded, feeling resolved for the first time in a long time.

"Okay? Okay, what? You'll forgive me?" His voice cracked.

"I will."

He sobbed in relief and hugged me. "I love you, and I'll spend the rest of my life proving that to you. I swear." His embrace got tighter the longer I stayed quiet.

"I love you, too. Please just be honest with me. If you have a moment, just *tell* me, and we can work through it. I know—I know how hard it is." I stumbled on my words. It was humbling, forgiving someone. The heaviness I'd felt in my heart only moments before, dissipated into something beautiful. I felt stronger, more in tune with him. I understood the embarrassment failing had caused him.

He hugged me tight, squeezing twice. "We're going home," he said into my hair.

"Tonight?" I was so tired, I could barely keep my eyes open.

He pulled his phone out, clicking away as I yawned. "We depart in two hours." He continued typing on his phone, not phased in the least about getting us home after all we'd been through.

"But it's so late. Wouldn't you rather sleep here and leave tomorrow?"

"No. I'm getting you out of this place. We're going home, and sleeping in my bed. In my house, where I know it's safe."

"What about Lena and Steele?" I asked.

"He's taking care of her. I just texted him."

"Okay . . . but—"

"No buts, baby. I want us to go home."

The sun filtering through the cracks in the blinds made its way through my closed eyelids. I squinted and stretched, and dull pain pulsated through my spine. My back felt shredded and stiff. I rolled over, throwing my legs up near the headboard trying to stretch it further.

"You look beautiful." Conner's deep voice startled me.

"Geez! Let a girl wake up before you do that!"

"Sorry." He smiled. "Can you wake up like that every morning from here on out?"

"No."

"No?"

"No, because if I did, my feet would be over your head, and my thighs on top of your face."

He winked. "Those are facts."

I shook my head, and rolled my eyes. "You're in a good mood, considering." I pushed my body into a sitting position, my feet dangling above the floor.

"Not in a good mood, just happy you're safe. Besides, I like you waking up here." He brought a coffee cup to the bedside table and knelt between my legs. "What if you woke up here every morning?"

I wasn't conscious enough for him to drop bombs like that on me. "You mean, like move in?"

"Yeah. Why not?"

"For one thing, we almost broke up last night." I hated to dwell on something so negative, but the fact remained.

His barely-there smile broke my heart all over again. He nodded, like he understood my reasoning, but disappointment remained in his eyes. He stood and patted my bare legs, before heading back toward the kitchen. "It's cool. I get it."

I wanted to rush after him and apologize for being so frank, but I didn't. I took my time getting dressed, and decided a little time apart would be good for us. That way, we could both collect our thoughts. Everything had been so overwhelming the past couple of days. It would do us both some good to be alone with our feelings for a day or two.

After brushing my teeth, I met him in the kitchen. "Hey. I'm going to head home. Thank you for—"

"You're not going home." He interrupted me and turned from the sink. His chest bare; a pair of basketball shorts hanging low from his hips. I wanted to smile from how desirable he looked, especially with both his hands resting casually on the counter behind him.

"Why not?"

"Are you fucking serious? You were literally in danger less than twenty-four hours ago. I'm not letting you out of my sight until that bastard is officially behind bars. As in staying there for a long time with no mention of bailing out."

I blew out a frustrated breath. He wasn't exactly thinking irrational. "When you put it like that," I stopped, not finishing the rest of my sentence.

"I'm putting it like that. I know you want some space. I can tell. But you're going to do it with me around, in the same house. Sorry." He shrugged.

He wasn't sorry. Not in the least.

"Can we go to my house to get some of my stuff then?" I conceded.

"Absolutely." He grinned.

CHAPTER 17
CONNER

RICHARD CALLED me not long after the first fight in New York. I hadn't had a chance to speak with him after the fight because of the incident with Willow. He congratulated me, and told me he saw a bright future with the league.

I talked to Steele about what that meant. I only admitted it to him, but I wasn't sure how far I wanted to take my career in fighting. It hadn't even been an option a year ago, and now I was approaching a six-figure deal for using my fists. Considering all that had happened in my life since I began my journey with the AFL, I wasn't sure it was worth it. Hell, I didn't know much of anything, other than I wanted Willow. I needed her.

"I know you don't want to talk about it." Willow stood to the right of her car, arms crossed. "But I feel like something is bothering you."

Rolling out from under her car, I looked up at her, flat on my back.

She'd sworn something was rattling underneath her vehicle, but everything seemed intact. Of course, me telling her that it hadn't made a noise when I drove it, only pissed her off. It was the truth, but I wanted her safe no matter what, so checking everything I knew to check was a must.

"I'm cool, babe." Grabbing my flashlight, I intended on rolling back under, when she stepped between me and the car. Looking up at her, I smiled. "I can't find the problem if you don't let me look. Or, if you want, you can strip for me, and we can make one of my fantasies a reality."

"Maybe some other time." She plopped her ass on my abdomen, and placed her hands on my chest. I grunted at the loss of air. "You don't talk about your training. And you haven't said one word about the whole Mikey situation. The space between us is growing, Conner, and I'm afraid you're going to . . ."

"You're afraid I'm going to what?" I didn't like where the conversation was going. Frustration grew deep in my gut. She'd been the one who had wanted space. All I'd done was give it to her.

"I don't know." She shrugged. "Grow tired of me? Pick up and leave behind the opportunity you have with the AFL?" She leaned back, and a small patch of skin showed between her T-shirt and cotton shorts. "I'm sorry, but I do think about you being tempted to drink. I know that pisses you off when I say that, but you're worrying me," she said, reeling me back into the conversation I didn't want to have. "I don't know what you're thinking, and it scares me."

I grabbed her backside, then lifted her above my head and to her feet. She stayed silent, yet grabbed my hands and helped me up. I paced back and forth. My thoughts were not becoming any clearer, but it was helping my urge to walk away. I gathered myself as best I could. Her doubting me while I doubted myself hurt, and I didn't know why. Everything she'd said had been true. Her calling me out on it wasn't unreasonable, but I was used to working things out on my own. Answering to someone else about my feelings and why I felt them was foreign to me.

I blew out a frustrated breath and turned to face her. She stood in the same spot I'd left her looking miserable. I hated that I had the ability to make her sad. It only added to my emotional insecurities.

"Look, you're the one who wanted space," I said. "I was simply giving that to you the best way I knew how. I'm sorry if you took that as me ignoring you."

"I know I said that, but I never wanted to push you away." She shook her head. "I only wanted to attempt to place my emotions and my thoughts in a neutral zone. Everything happened so fast, you know? It was overwhelming, and I just wanted to work it all out."

I pushed my hands through my hair, then remembered they were dirty. I grabbed a towel off my work bench to clean them. "I get that, but telling me you don't want to be with me pretty much killed me. I mean, if you don't want to be here, what are we doing?"

"Conner, I *do* want to be here. That's not the same thing as wanting space to be able to think clearly. I love you."

"And I love you, Willow. I want to show you that. I want to tell you that. I want you to know how much I love you; so much so, that when you go to bed without me at night, I can't sleep because not only is my body aching for you, my soul is too. That's how I feel about you. I physically feel numb when I'm not with you. Like my body doesn't work right, unless you're beside me. Like my heart isn't pumping correctly unless it's in sync with yours."

"I feel the same. I never want to be without you, but I can't shake the feeling that something is wrong. Like you're secretly doubting us, or maybe yourself? Whatever it is, it's worrying me." She leaned against the workbench.

"Please talk to me."

I wiped my hands on my jeans once more, and walked over to her. I reached for her and she didn't resist. "I don't like not knowing why Mikey tried to hurt you." I squeezed her hands once. "I sit here day in and day out, wondering if I'm losing what makes me strong. I know you doubt me sometimes, but Willow—" I brought both her hands to my face, guiding them from my ears to my lips. I wanted her to feel my words as I spoke them. "I know I messed up in Vegas. I know I'm the reason for you almost being injured in New York. I know I hurt you, and I know that is hard for you to forget."

I pulled her along with me, as I backed up and took a seat on a stool. Placing my hands on her hips, I turned her around and sat her in my lap. I spoke into her shoulder as I admitted what had taken over my thoughts—to the point I couldn't sleep—since it had happened. "The truth is, I feel guilty. Everything negative thing that has happened to you has been because of me. I've hurt you and I've put you in danger."

She tilted her head to the side, then rubbed my jaw with her forehead. Hot breaths tickled my cheek as she kissed her way to my ear. I squeezed her middle and kept my arms wrapped firmly around her, caging her in, keeping her firmly planted on my lap.

"I want you to understand, even though things aren't perfect right now, I will fight for us with everything I have. I will never give up on us. I promise." I grabbed her pinky, and linked it with mine. "There is nothing that will ever come between us again. Not my thoughts, not an ex, and not my drinking." I kissed her thumb, solidifying my word.

She rose and turned around, facing me. Placing one leg on each side of mine, she spread her legs wide, pushing herself up into my lap. She wrapped her legs around me, locking her ankles around my waist, inching her ass closer, until she'd closed the gap between our bodies. My body roused, coming to life as her ass sunk lower, giving me all her weight. I closed my eyes at the feel of her.

Neither of us spoke as she wrapped her arms around my neck, using the leverage to inch closer. So close, I could feel the outline of her center through her flimsy shorts. My body burned with desire. Grabbing two handfuls of her ass, I started a slow, methodical rock, sliding her heated core across my dick.

"Don't ever feel guilty for something you have no control over. Mikey did what he did," she said, continuing to follow my lead, her heels digging into my back when she wanted to be closer. "He's in jail now, and once his trial is over, he'll be back in prison." She brought her lips to my jaw, barely skimming across my skin. Her warm breath caressed my cheek light as a feather. "I believe you when you tell me you won't drink anymore, it's just that—" Her back arched in my arms, her face almost even with my own. "I know what it's like. Craving something. I know what it's like, chasing that first high. It's always in the back of your mind, taunting you—teasing you. The moment something doesn't go right, it's right there, begging you to come back, so you can at least forget for a little while."

I gritted my teeth at the friction we were creating, and blew out a heavy breath. "It won't. I won't let it."

"It will. It always does. *I* still think about it, Conner." She groaned and moved her hips in circles over my erection.

I tugged on her hair with one hand, pulling her head back, while the other slid down the back of her shorts, grabbing on to her bare ass cheek. "The reason either of us did what we did, I'll never fully understand. But what I do know is you were never part of the equation. I've done the math. Adding alcohol in only subtracts you." I nipped at her chin. "In my mind, no matter what kind of high I gain, in the end, I will lose you. And I'm not willing to let that happen. Ever."

I looked up just in time to catch the first tear spill from the corner of her eye, quickly disappearing into her hair. It broke me and gave me peace at the same time. I let go of her hair and her face was level with mine. I ran the pad of my thumb over her cheek as a second tear fell.

"You made me cry." She wrapped her arms around my neck. "I hate you."

I wanted to lick every last tear track on her cheeks. I wanted them to disappear. I wanted them to have never been there in the first place.

"You love me, baby. And I love you." I kissed her neck. Once, twice, three times, while she ran her fingers through my hair.

Leaning into her body, I pushed us up from the stool, and gently carried her over and set her down on the tool bench. It didn't occur to me to go slow. Getting inside the woman I loved was the only thought I had. That, and knowing no matter what happened next week—or next year, or five years from now—I was never letting her go.

She pulled her T-shirt and sports bra off. Then leaned from side to side as I helped her out of her cotton shorts and panties. She sat completely naked in front of me, spread wide. No lingerie, no makeup. She had never looked more beautiful to me.

Her hands moved quickly, discarding my T-shirt. Then her feet followed suit, pushing my shorts down my hips. In one swift movement, she scooted to the end of the bench and leaned back, wrapping her legs around my hips. Grabbing hold of myself, I guided my way inside her, finding heaven on earth. I could have wept at how magnificent she felt. Her hips synced with mine; the transition so smooth, it was like she was made specifically for me. As if our body, mind, and spirit were one.

Her sighs and moans drove me half mad. I went from thoroughly enjoying myself, to not caring if I ever got off again, as long as she did. I leaned into her, wrapping my arms around her back. Taking her breast into my mouth, I sucked hard, causing her nipple to pucker. I licked around the areola, making her moan again as I continued to plunge into her deeper each time.

My gaze wondered to her face and I fell in love all over again. Willow's eyes were closed tight, as if she was experiencing so much pleasure, it was borderline pain. Her lips parted, and she let out shallow breaths, letting me know she was chasing her release. There was something about being present in that moment with her, watching her ride her own wave of ecstasy that had my insides twisting in so many knots, I didn't know if I'd ever be able to untangle them.

I brought my palms to either side of her face. My torso wasn't touching hers, but I wanted it like that. I wanted to watch her. She pulled, pushed, and tugged on my wrists, bringing her hips up to meet mine in what seemed like a million miles a second. In the past, I tried a total of two times to not come before my partner. Neither of those times worked. But this—this was something different. My body knew automatically that it was giving and wouldn't be receiving until Willow was limp in my arms.

"I love you." I hadn't wanted to interfere with her blissful state, but I couldn't help it. I needed her to know that I would die for her. I would work three jobs for her if it meant keeping a roof over her head. She had to know I understood what my past addiction would cost me if it raised its ugly head again, and from this point forward, I would never risk what I had with her for something as paltry as a drink.

When her breathing evened out, I focused on where our bodies met, watching as I pushed in and out, as deep as I could go, until I grunted out my own release.

Feeling a hundred pounds heavier, I limply fell atop her sweaty skin; the two of us still joined.

She wrapped her arms around me and squeezed me tightly, clearly having more energy than I had. "I love you, Conner. More than anything."

I rubbed her back, letting her words wash over me, comforting me after I'd laid my whole heart on the table for her, exposed. Every scar, every fear, every inconsistent beat, she'd seen. I closed my eyes, praying she'd still want it in the morning, after she had time to think about all I'd shown her. My scars told the story, and unfortunately, it was a messy one.

CHAPTER 18
WILLOW

"MOMMA, I'M HOME!" I yelled from the front door, knowing she was in the kitchen, whipping up my favorites because I was visiting. She couldn't resist.

Faster than I expected her to move, she was on me within seconds. Her arms engulfed my whole body, and she held on tighter than I remembered she could. I loved her hugs. She put every ounce of feeling she had into them. By the time she let go, I knew exactly how much she'd missed me.

I pulled the cute purple bag out from behind me. "Happy Mother's Day."

"Oh, Willow." She wiped her hands on her dish towel. "You didn't have to get me anything. Having you home is enough."

"I know. But I wanted to do something nice for you."

Tears rolled down her cheeks when she pulled the quilt from the bag. Her hands held it at one end as she unfolded it, so she could see the whole thing. I knew I had nailed it, and it made me feel good.

She covered her mouth with her hand, shocked and grateful at the same time. "Sweetie. I don't know what to say."

"Isn't it cool? I thought you could put it on my old bed, since you needed a new one."

My mom's eyes never left the quilt. She ran her hand over each picture of us, as if she were going over every memory in her mind. I couldn't help but get a little emotional myself. We'd been through a lot. Most of it hell, and all of it my fault. But there were moments in between where we just loved each other. There were times when my mom was my best friend—my *only* friend—and there were times where I made her proud.

"This is the best present I've ever received. Thank you so much." I walked eagerly into her outstretched arms. "I know you already know this, but I'm so proud of you. Of the woman you've become."

"Momma, stop. You're going to make me cry." I kissed her cheek.

"Oh, all right. Let's eat. That will calm us down." She folded the quilt and I followed her to the kitchen.

My mouth watered when I saw her homemade quiche. She'd made my favorite, on *her* day. God, I loved her. As I gathered the plates, my insides pinched with guilt, knowing Conner was training—working his ass off for another opportunity. He wasn't reminiscing with his mom about the good ole days, nor was he getting his favorite meal made for him with love.

"What are you thinking about? You're frowning," Mom said while bringing the napkins to the table.

"Conner."

"What about him?"

"He doesn't have what I have, you know?" I bowed my head, thinking about my past. "Like me—he's made mistakes, and his mom isn't in his life."

"That's awful." She patted my hand. "From everything you've told me about him, he seems like a wonderful young man."

"He is, Mom. He's loving and loyal. He always puts me first, no matter what's going on. I just get so pissed off that he's had to go through most of his life with little to no support. And I can't help but think about what I put you through—the bad decisions I've made—yet you've never disowned me. You've always loved me, even when I didn't love myself."

"And I always will, sweetie." She rubbed my arm and pulled me in for another hug. "I know you said you were taking it slow, but I'd like to meet Conner one of these days. You said it yourself, you love him, right?"

"I do." I smiled, not even realizing it, until I relaxed my cheeks.

"I can see that." She grinned. "What's the harm in your mother meeting the man you love?"

"None, I guess." I shrugged. "I just feel like I should tread lightly where moms are concerned, you know?"

"I get it." She nodded. "Maybe just a dinner?"

"Okay, we can do that."

I stayed at Mom's longer than I planned and even though she swore she wouldn't bring him up again, she couldn't stop herself. We talked about Conner most of our time together, but I didn't mind. She was excited and honestly, I was too. Being loved felt good.

When I entered Conner's backyard, it was nearly ten o'clock.

"Hey, guys."

Steele and Conner paused their conversation, as Conner stood up and greeted me with a kiss on the lips. "How was your mom?"

"She's really good. She loved the quilt."

"I knew she would. You worry too much about shit that doesn't matter." Steele and I both laughed, even though it wasn't exactly a compliment.

"What have you guys been grilling?" I could still feel the heat radiating off the metal lid.

"Meat," Steele said, flicking a toothpick from one side of his mouth to the other. "All the meat."

"Kind of late for dinner." I ran a hand over the knotted muscles of Conner's back. "You need rest." I massaged the hard lumps at the base of his neck.

He made a sound normally saved for a private setting. "I wanted to wait for you to get home."

"Richard is coming in for this fight," Steele mentioned from the patio chair.

"Doesn't he usually?" I'd never met him formally, but he normally made an appearance where a lot of money would be concerned.

"Yeah," Steele answered. "But this time he should have another contract in hand. If Payne wins, it could change his life."

"He's going to win," I said with no hesitation.

"I just want to make sure you're ready mentally," Steele said, and nodded toward Conner. "I know you don't like the fame shit, but that's part of it. You saw in New York—" He closed his mouth, taking in Conner's facial expression.

"I get it," Conner clipped. "I'll do what I gotta do."

"I've been thinking," I said to change the direction of bad memories. "I've seen on social media how curious people are about you. The one interview we did kept most of them at bay. Maybe if we did another one, where I kept the questions focused on the sport and your future inside the cage, it would tamp down some of the eagerness about the mystery of who you are personally."

"I don't want to do that. Look," he blew out a frustrated breath, "I know keeping myself private only adds to the curiosity, but I can't have the general public knowing what I've gone through. I just can't."

"Okay." I eyed Steele, letting him know our conversation was over.

"We'll do a light workout tomorrow," Steele added. "Then, it's fucking game time. You got this, man."

"Thanks." Conner leaned into me and kissed my cheek. "I'm going to hit the shower." Silence fell over the backyard as he went inside the house.

"I'm worried," I admitted as soon as I heard the click from the sliding glass door.

"Me too," Steele agreed. "I kind of feel responsible. I mean, I pushed him into this, and Willow—he's not ready. Not mentally."

"I know. What do I do?" I asked.

"Just be by his side. He's doing this for you, not for himself."

"Me?" I pressed my hand to my chest. "I'm very careful about his fights and my opinion of them." Conner was aware of my distaste for seeing him hurt, but I was supportive. I kept myself in the loop, always wanting to learn more, so that he felt like he had someone in his corner. Someone who loved him, no matter the outcome.

"He wants a future with you, doll. He wants you taken care of."

"I can take care of myself. I've been doing it for years."

"I know you can. He knows you can. But he wants to do it," he said. "He's never shown me his true potential before meeting you.

He's going to blow this sport up, Willow. I just hope you're ready, because he isn't. And trust me," he leaned forward, resting his forearms on the table, "he will need you when all the noise gets too loud." For the first time since I'd met him, I saw shadows of doubt behind Steele's eyes. His vulnerability was hard to witness, especially when it had to do with my boyfriend.

I closed the distance between us and rubbed his shoulder, feeling like he needed comfort. "Hey," I said. "I got him. I promise, whatever happens, I've got him."

He scooted his chair back and stood. "God, if that douchebag doesn't marry you, I will."

I giggled and brought him in for a hug. "Let's not get ahead of ourselves. We've barely made it to the point where I'll pee in front of him."

"Damn, girl. You sure know how to kill a mood." His right eyebrow rose just a hair. "Or start one. Now, I'm picturing you with your pants down." He made his way toward the side of the house, whistling.

"Goodnight, pervert." I walked to the patio door, chuckling. I was so glad Conner had him. I believed in quality over quantity where friends were concerned, and Steele was a good one. I knew he loved my man, and would do anything for him. For me, it lessened my load somewhat, knowing there was at least one more person Conner could count on for things I didn't understand.

Conner was setting his alarm when I finished brushing my teeth. I slid under the covers and curled my legs so that my backside snuggled perfectly into his body.

"I love you," he said as he wrapped an arm around me.

I hugged his arm tighter around my waist. "My mom wants to meet you."

"Oh yeah?"

"Yeah. She's mentioned it twice now, so unless you want me to suffer twenty questions every time I talk to her, you're going to have to take one for the team."

He pulled on my shoulder until I turned around, so that we were facing each other. Darkness surrounded us, but I could see the blue in his eyes from the moonlight steaming in through the window. His hand brushed the side of my hair softly. "Meeting your mom is no hardship. She's a part of you."

"I'd like to meet yours too one day."

"Willow, I can't—we've talked about this before, and I give you the same answer each time." He rolled onto his back, and placed his palms over his eyes.

"But you haven't tried to contact her in so long, maybe she's changed her mind."

He sighed. "Look, I know what you're trying to do. And I appreciate the fact that you care. But—"

"But what?" I asked.

"I'm trying to say this and not sound like a dick."

"Go on." He was for sure going to sound like a dick.

"You have to leave it alone. What's done is done. It puts me on edge when you talk about it. Stop. Please?"

I frowned, knowing no matter what I said, he wasn't going to hear it. Feeling defeated, I rolled away from him.

"Are you pissed?"

"No. Just tired," I said, pulling the blankets up under my chin. "Goodnight."

I was pissed and hurt. But more than that, I was annoyed with myself for feeling pissed and hurt. I was being such a girl. A selfish one at that. Just because I didn't know the ins and outs of Conner's relationship with his mother, didn't mean his reasons for keeping me in the dark weren't warranted.

CHAPTER 19
CONNER

"STOP FUCKIN' around, and get it done! Quick." Steele's voice echoed from my right side, as I took another large gulp of water.

The fight had already lasted two rounds. I gritted my teeth in annoyance. There was no way around it. If I did decide to sign the contract, Willow would have to be closer to me in future fights, or I'd have to leave her ass at home, because I couldn't concentrate knowing she was down in the crowd where I couldn't get to her fast enough if danger arose. Flashbacks from the night Mikey accosted her broke through the mental wall I'd worked so hard to create prior to my second contracted fight. Most of the time, focusing was one of my strong suits. It wasn't tonight though.

"Get her," I ordered, never making eye contact with him. Instead, I kept my gaze trained on Willow. I had two of Steele's clients surrounding her, hoping the extra security would make her feel safe.

"I'm watching her. Dammit, man. Keep your mind here."

"I'm here. Just get her."

"I'll send Gage."

"If he touches her, I'll kill him." I was only halfway joking. I knew that little fucker would take whatever shot he had at making moves on a beautiful woman.

"Got it. Now go. End this, so we can celebrate."

I nodded once, finally feeling secure enough to not focus on her. Since Willow would be making her way to me, I knew I had just enough time to choke out my opponent before she made it cage side.

Once I was back in the center of the cage, I wasted no time taking my challenger to the ground. One leg lock, and an arm hold later, I had him. I squeezed once, and held it as tight as I could. My legs brought him closer to me for a firmer grip. I pulled my right fist toward me with my left hand, closing the gap between my forearm and his neck. Cutting off his air, I felt his head lull, causing the referee to call the fight.

I stood and looked toward my corner. Willow wasn't there yet. With the crowd screaming and chanting, I blocked out the noise until I saw her being escorted by Gage down the front aisle. I knew he'd find a way to touch her. That asshole.

The ref called me back to the center of the cage for the official announcement. I followed his instructions, and once my name was called as the winner, I exited the cage, not caring about anything other than having Willow in my arms.

She wrapped her arms around my sweaty body. "Conner, I'm fine."

"I couldn't keep my head in the game."

"I know. I was worried there for a minute."

I should have felt bad for ruining her perfectly put together outfit, or her hair, but I didn't. I just needed to hold her, more for my own well-being than hers.

"I'm so proud of you." Her smile was infectious, and her words gave me more confidence than ever before. She was proud of me. *Proud.*

I kissed her, pouring every ounce of adrenaline I had into it. I was so overcome with emotion, I hadn't noticed the flashes from the cameras, until she pulled away and ducked her head into my chest.

Grabbing her hand, I tugged her toward the locker room to safety. Uncertainty filled my bones with each step. What would they say about us? About her? Were they going to print those pictures? I still hadn't heard a word about the investigation since Mikey had been arrested.

"Dude!" Gage said as he entered the room with Steele.

"Who were those photographers? Are they from the newspaper?" I asked, wanting to know exactly what outlet they'd be published in.

"Chill out, man. Those are Richard's photogs. They print for him and a couple of national magazines. Most of them are reputable. He'll go over all that at the press conference."

"Press conference?" No one had mentioned a press conference.

"Yeah, he'll announce your offer after he speaks with—"

"Conner fucking Payne." Richard appeared in a suit that probably cost more than Willow's whole wardrobe. He was followed by his asshat son, Preston, his daughter, Navie, and what appeared to be two bodyguards.

I pushed Willow behind me, feeling like I needed to protect her, yet not knowing why. Fortunately, for once, she went willingly. "Richard."

"I knew you had it in you." He pulled an envelope out of his suit pocket. "You want an audience for this?"

I glanced around the room, taking in everyone from Steele to Navie. The bodyguards remained stiff, with no emotion on their faces. In fact, they looked just ahead like they'd been instructed to do so. Preston's perfectly gelled hair made him look weak to me. Gage seemed enamored. I knew, like me, he was working his ass off for the opportunity. Steele was perfectly composed; relaxed, even.

Navie seemed a million miles away, but smiled at both me and Willow. It was the first time I realized how pretty she was. Her body was lean, but muscular, as anyone could see, due to her black pantsuit fitting like a glove. I looked to Steele, hoping he would pick up the conversation slack, but to no avail. He might as well have been a cartoon character with heart-shaped eyeballs.

"We're doing this here?" I asked.

Richard grinned. "We are. And as soon as you sign, we're going to announce it."

"Why so soon?" I questioned him. "No one mentioned anything to me about a formal announcement." Willow grabbed my hand in support.

"This is how I do things. You sign, I announce." He handed me the contract. "I'm a busy man, Conner. This is the most efficient way."

I took the envelope from him, and took a seat on the old, worn-out couch in the corner. My eyes widened as I read over the contract.

Holy shit. One million dollars?

I refocused my eyes, thinking I wasn't seeing the numbers on the page correctly. Willow's hand landed on my arm, but I couldn't look away from the page. All my thoughts floated around in my brain, continuously coming at me from all sides.

One million dollars for seven fights. I glanced up at Steele, feeling like a fool. I had no idea he made this kind of money. Hell, he made way more than what I was being offered, considering he'd been fighting for years. And I'd been living off four grand a month, thinking I was really doing something.

"Conner?" Willow's voice broke through my thoughts.

I glanced at her, then back to the page. As her body leaned into mine, so that she could see what I was reading, pride swelled in my gut. God, I couldn't believe it. One year. Seven fights. And enough money to take care of her the way she deserved.

"I'm assuming you're good with the amount?" Richard asked, speaking loud enough for the whole room to hear.

"I want to talk to Steele," I said, not answering his question. "Alone."

"Very well." Richard nodded. "I'll wait in the booth. Don't take too long. Time is money. Remember, we have to make the announcement that you'll be joining the AFL."

"Let me take a look." Steele approached the couch after Richard and his party left the room. "If you don't mind me seeing what he's offering."

I handed him the packet and collapsed back onto the sofa. I still hadn't changed, or even showered. The tape on my hands seemed tighter, as if my knuckles were about to burst through. Willow noticed and began to unwrap them.

"Don't sign if you have any doubts," she counseled.

I looked up at Steele, who was vigorously reading over every word. "It's not *doubt* I worry about."

"What is it?" she asked.

"I have you to think about too. That money—we will be set." I brought my hand to my face, placing my index finger and thumb on the bridge of my nose. "But as you know, I'm not comfortable with losing my privacy. Not to mention, you will lose yours too."

"Don't base your decision on me." She rubbed my arm. "Do you want to do this?"

"Everything I do in life from here on out will be based on you." Her head tilted to the side in surprise. "I want—" Steele had made his way over to an oak desk in the corner. I lowered my voice and continued. "I want to marry you. I want to live the rest of my life knowing you're mine, and that whatever happens, we're doing it together."

Her eyes widened, and she smiled. "I want that too."

"Yeah? So, you'll marry me?"

She laughed with glee. "Yes. I will marry you!" Jumping in my lap, she kissed me before I could respond.

My hands—one still taped—gripped her ass as hard as I could. I pulled her into me tighter than ever before, knowing if we both hadn't been so happy, I probably would have hurt her. I couldn't help it. Everything in my body needed her to be as close as I could get her.

"You guys done yet?" Steele interrupted. "Or should I leave the room too?"

"We're getting married," Willow announced.

He grinned. "Figured, since I heard the proposal."

"I don't give a fuck who heard it." I beamed, keeping my eyes trained on Willow's. "What do you think about the contract?" I hated to talk business, when all I wanted to do was take her back to our hotel, and show her how happy she'd just made me.

"It's a good start."

"Start?"

"For your first year. Next year, depending on how much money you bring in and how many fights you win—which better be seven— I'd say you could get four or five times this amount."

Willow screeched, causing me to jump. I chuckled when she covered her mouth with both hands like a child. I hugged her again before I stood to sign the contract.

"One thing." Steele held up a finger. "He wants you to move to Vegas for training."

My smile fell. "Is that something he would reconsider? I'd rather keep things the way they are, and train with you."

"Let's see. I'll go get him."

Steele walked out, leaving me and Willow alone for the first time since the fight had ended. I wrapped my arm around her shoulders, pulling her in tight.

"I don't mind moving, if we have to," she said.

"I appreciate that, baby, but I don't want to." I kissed the top of her head, trying to calm my nerves, worried Richard wouldn't give in.

"Conner, don't lose this opportunity because of it."

"I don't want you to be away from your mom." I couldn't ask her to leave her mother. Not when she was such a huge part of her life.

"We will work it out."

Steele returned, along Gage, Richard, Preston, Navie, and his two bodyguards. "I assume you've made your decision."

"One thing," Steele cut in. "He doesn't want to move. He can train with me, until two weeks before each fight. At that time, he'll fly to Vegas. That should be enough time for your trainers, doctors, and anyone else you want him to work with to formulate your plans."

Richard eyed Steele, as if they were the only two people in the room. "So, basically, he wants what you have."

The tension in the room was thick. It felt like we were watching a duel from the Old West. Steele seemed his easy-going self, yet his gaze was stern. Business like. And Richard appeared almost amused, but lethal.

Steele pulled a pen from his desk. "Basically, yeah. I'll change it here." He jotted down the changes and handed the papers back to me.

It read word for word what he'd said to Richard. I nodded, letting him know I agreed and he handed the pen to Richard. The room was silent. Richard grabbed the paper from my hands and walked with purpose to the desk. My grip tightened on Willow's waist as the man signing my future pay checks placed his initials beside the changes.

"Do we have a deal then?" Richard asked.

"Yes, sir," I said, signing my name to the bottom of the page.

CHAPTER 20
WILLOW

"I'LL JOIN you if you don't mind," Navie said, as I excused myself to use the restroom. It had been twenty minutes since Conner had officially entered the AFL, and they were chatting about how the press conference would go.

"Of course." I smiled. "You can show me where it is." Once we'd made it out of the room, and away from the men, I hugged her.

"I'm so glad you're doing okay. I've been worried about you," she said.

"Me? Girl, I've been worried about you. I still can't believe all that happened. I'll never be able to repay you."

She chuckled. "Oh, please! I wish I would have been able to do more damage."

"I've never seen a woman so fierce. I was super impressed with your moves."

"Thanks. I've had a few lessons in secret. My dad knows, but he thinks I'm just working out to stay in shape. Because that's what ladies do, stay fit to look good for men." She rolled her eyes.

"That is so sexist. I mean, doesn't he see how talented you are?" I asked as we entered the restroom.

"No." She sighed. "He won't even give me a chance to show him."

I exited the stall, noticing she hadn't moved from the sink since we'd entered.

"Is everything okay?" I asked while washing my hands.

"Perfect." She rolled her eyes. "I'm in a bathroom fixing my makeup, while Preston is rubbing elbows with my dad's business partners, and my dad—well, he just made millions by signing Payne."

"I'm sorry." I hadn't known her very long, but I could tell from what she'd already shared, her life was probably a walking poster board on how money didn't equate happiness.

"For?" she questioned, dabbing two fingers of color on her lips.

I dried my hands with the fancy towel. "I've debated even telling you this, but I saw the video."

"Which one?" She stopped fixing her makeup and stared ahead, looking at me through the mirror.

I wasn't aware there was more than one. "The one where your father tells you point blank you'll stay behind a desk in the AFL."

"Oh." Her face fell, and she slipped the compact back in her purse. "That one's a classic. But if you really want to be offended, I'll bring you down to his headquarters. There, you can see me working in the front office, answering my dad's phone calls, and taking messages for the fighters." She smiled sarcastically. "It isn't all bad, I guess. Sometimes, I mess with the cage bunnies who call looking for the guys."

I laughed and slung my arm around her neck, as we walked out toward the area where the press conference would go down. I loved Navie. I loved how strong and intelligent she seemed. I knew there were going to be plenty of girls' nights in our future.

Finding my man just outside the media room, I made a beeline to him. I was so worried about Conner. We'd just made two life-altering decisions in less than an hour, and I hadn't even had time to check on him. It was more than obvious he was nervous, which made me nervous.

My stomach was in knots waiting for everything to start, especially when Conner took his seat next to Richard. I did my part and winked at him, trying to reassure him.

Media people started piling in, one after another, until the whole room was packed so tight, I started sweating from all the body heat.

Navie's brother took a seat next to his father, with Steele on the other side of Conner. There were four other men in expensive suits who finished out the panel, but I didn't know who they were.

Flashes from every direction started going off like fireworks. Conner squinted. I wanted to approach the stage and hug him, but I settled for clasping my hands together as Richard began speaking.

"Thank you all for being here." Richard's voice was deep and thick. It carried through the room, as if he were a professional announcer. "This is an exciting time for the AFL, as we are expanding our family today. Conner Payne will be signing a one-year deal. We will take a few questions, but as usual, this will be short and sweet."

An AFL ball cap sat just to Conner's left. I assumed they were expecting him to put it on at the end. I knew that wasn't going to happen. I only hoped the media blitz went well, and Conner was able to answer their questions quickly and efficiently, so we could get out of there.

A scrawny man with khakis and a blue button-up stood with the first question. I glanced at Navie, who sat perfectly poised, her legs crossed and her hands in her lap. She'd obviously attended a few of these before.

"Payne, I've followed you since your first fight. What do you think has influenced you the most with your ground work? Is that something you lean toward because it's natural?" Scrawny dude sat back down, ready to take the notes from Conner's answer.

Conner cleared his throat and looked to Steele before answering. "I feel comfortable on the ground. I'm stronger in my legs, and I'm patient. I don't mind waiting someone out."

The crowd snickered. I smiled too, because even though I knew he'd rather chew his right arm off than talk to a bunch of strangers, he was charming with his response, and he didn't even know it.

"Richard, will Conner be the only new addition to the family this season?" a woman asked from the back.

"We're not releasing any information about the family's expansion, other than Conner at this time," Richard answered, after taking a sip of his water.

"Conner! Do you know who your first fight will be with?" asked someone else from the back.

"No." Conner's legs were bouncing under the table. I wanted so badly to crawl under there and calm them.

An older gentleman threw a question at him without being called on. "Will Trevor Steele be your trainer? How will he have time to train full time, plus fight his own bouts?"

"I'm—"

Preston, Richard's son interrupted Conner. "It's undecided at this stage who will train Conner. Same goes for where that will take place."

Steele grinned from the side, but Conner did not. I could see plain on his face Preston was pissing him off. So could everyone else in the room, which I was sure would be splattered across the front page of the sports section tomorrow. Conner's nostrils flared wide as he stared Preston down, letting everyone in the room know he didn't appreciate being interrupted. I cleared my throat, hoping he'd hear me. My subtle interference gained his attention. He nodded and reset.

"Payne, everyone wants to know. Are you single?" asked some blonde bimbo who'd clearly gotten her job as a sports reporter because of her DD's. *Gag.*

Conner's brows pinched together, and he scowled. My insides tickled with glee as he ignored her out of protection for our privacy. After he looked away, clearly dismissing her stupid question, Navie snorted from my side. The room became so quiet I could hear the tick from the clock in the corner.

A young male reporter in the front row stepped up next. "Now that you're under contract, what sponsor deals are you expecting?"

"I don't expect anything," Conner replied.

Chatter filled the room, with each reporter fighting for the next question, until a strong female voice filtered from the corner of the room, drowning out all other voices. Recognizing the voice, I looked over, shocked.

"Do you think because you've murdered someone before," Dana said, her voice strong and clear, "along with the time you served in prison, the lack of empathy on your part will contribute to your mindset in terms of legally hurting someone professionally?"

I gasped. First, I was outraged at Dana's callousness, and secondly, confused by the personal information she knew about Conner.

After a couple of seconds of silence, the media in the room began snapping photos, yelling out into the room, one right after the other, asking if the allegations were true. Beyond a hand-full absurd questions, I couldn't distinguish anything other than rambunctious shouting.

My gaze quickly found Conner; his face the palest I'd ever seen it. My body trembled taking in his hunched shoulders; his deepest secret revealed for all to judge. Out of instinct, I moved toward the stage.

It was as if I was in a dream. My surroundings; blurred images, yet the image of my boyfriend—alone and needing protection, was as crisp as a new dollar bill. I could literally feel his emotions only by the sight of him. The crinkles at his eyes. The forward bend of his neck. The way his chest rose and fell in cadence. Flashes from the cameras continued their assault on Conner's body, each one appearing like a gun shot, sucking the life out of him.

I reached him within moments, and grabbed his arm. Pulling him up, I led him down the steps and into the only room I could find with a door. Steele followed, closing and locking it.

"Hey." I stepped in front of Conner, trying to get his attention. His shoulders slumped forward, regret and embarrassment clear on his face. He didn't respond. "Sweetie, look at me."

"Man, come on. That bitch was just trying to get a rise out of you for whatever rag she is writing for. I told you this might happen. All we have to do is release a statement, and tomorrow, it will be some other poor fucker."

"That *bitch* is going to get sued," I ranted. "I don't know how Dana found out about your past." No wonder I hadn't heard from her. She'd been ignoring my emails, but I had so much going on with Conner and his career, I almost welcomed the reprieve. "I swear, Conner, I didn't tell her a thing. I never even mentioned you, except the one interview I did. And that was—"

"*That's* Dana?" He barely whispered it. Had I not been paying attention, I probably wouldn't have even heard him.

"Yes. She's been shady lately. I wanted to tell you more, but I didn't want you to worry about my job, when you had all this going on." I opened my arms and gestured around the room.

He closed his eyes and shook his head. "Her name is not Dana."

Confused, I asked. "What do you mean?"

Loud knocking came from the other side of the door, along with voices I didn't recognize. I worried how we were going to get out of there with so much commotion. Conner leaned up against the wall, looking more defeated than ever before. Panic seized me, causing me to feel off kilter. I placed my hand on the side of the wall to help keep my balance.

"Her name is Cyndi Hanky. She's the mother of the boy I killed."

Steele and I looked at each other before turning back to Conner. My guts clenched. What he said couldn't be true. Instantly, guilt circled my gut, making me feel responsible for not paying more attention to the bad feelings I'd had toward Dana, or Cyndi—whatever her name was. I should have realized something was off because she'd been so inter-ested in him. Instead, I chalked her infatuation up to him being new meat for the AFL.

"I have to get out of here." Conner moved with purpose toward the door. "I have to go."

"Hold up. Let me clear the way, and you guys can—" Steele tried to help.

"No." Conner gritted his teeth. "Move." He shoved Steele's shoul-der. "Get Willow back to the hotel."

"Conner, wait! Don't leave me." I wanted to help fix things. Even if I didn't know how, I knew he needed me.

"I'm sorry. I just need some time." He turned back to Steele. "Get her back safe."

I felt like grabbing onto his leg and making him drag me behind him. I wanted to beg him to let me go with him. "Steele?" I cried as Conner opened the door to a flash mob, and pushed his way through the crowd forcefully. All I saw was his back muscles contracting, his body outwardly panicking as he barreled through everyone standing in his way.

CHAPTER 21
CONNER

THE VIBRATION in my pocket startled me. My body jerked, and my lungs expanded as I took a deep breath and debated on reading the text messages. I knew they were from Willow, and I felt guilty ignoring them. Now that I'd made it to my final destination, I realized the last thing I wanted was for her to worry about me. I pulled the phone from my pocket, and saw I had multiple missed phone calls, along with a few text messages from both her and Steele.

Steele: Where are you? I can come to you.
Willow: Please tell me where you are. I love you.
Steele: Man, come on. It's going to be okay. We'll figure it out.
Willow: I'm getting worried. Call me. I love you.
Steele: Willow's worried and so am I. Just let us know you're okay.
Willow: Whatever you're thinking, just know I'm behind you. I will hold you up, support you, and be whatever you need me to be until the day I die, because you deserve it.
Willow: Be careful. And know that whatever happens, I'm here and I always will be.
Willow: And also, I really, really fucking hate you right now.

It was too early to knock on the door, so I sat across the street, staking out the place. I took in every square inch of the yard, and the way the fence was leaning on the left side of the house. I calculated the distance from my spot in my truck to the front porch. The house needed to be painted. It needed a new roof, and the grass was in desperate need of cutting. The house to the left was newly remodeled. The house on the right looked cookie-cutter.

I circled my lips with my index finger as I sat there, alone in silence, telling myself over and over that I'd done my time. I'd paid the price.

Punching my stirring wheel twice, I bent forward, feeling like collapsing from the weight of the world I'd created crashing down on me. Why did I need her forgiveness to move on with my life? It was like she held the key to my happiness, even though I had everything perfectly placed right in front of me for the taking.

As the sun came up, I leaned back in my seat, taking in the purple, yellow, orange, and red colors that all worked together in the sky. Picking my phone up, I sent off a text to ease Willow's concern.

Me: I'm okay. I just need some time. Don't worry, I'll call you later.
Willow: If you need anything, please tell me. I love you.

Placing my phone back in my pocket, I perched on the edge of my seat when a flicker of light came on from the living room window. The hue of darkness was barely visible anymore with the sunrise making its way into the sky.

I pulled the handle on the door of my pick up, and stepped outside for the first time in ten hours. The air was different. It smelled musty, and the mugginess of the scorched morning clogged my pours. I put one foot in front of the other, until I counted fifty-seven steps.

Eyes trained on the front window, I raised my numb hand, and knocked on the door. My blood pressure spiked, causing me to break out into a sweat. The top of my head was heated, and my legs felt wobbly. I was a grown man reduced to a small child, as the possibility of rejection stared me straight in the face.

One.
Two.
Three.

Four.

Five.

My mom answered the door appearing older, but mostly unchanged.

I stood unmoving, keeping my distance. My gaze followed the length of her body, unable to make eye contact for some reason. She wore the same pink robe I remembered all those years ago. It looked the same. She did too, other than the gray hair. She wore a gold ring with the tiniest rose in the middle on her right hand; one her mother had given her before she died. Her nails were painted a pale pink. She had dark, weary eyes, even though she'd just awakened from I assumed was a full night's rest.

"Conner." Her voice cracked.

At the sound of her voice, I glanced up. "I know you don't want to see me, but I . . ." All that time on the road, and I hadn't thought of one thing to say to her. My mind was blank. Pain and resentment had always been in the front of my mind when I thought of her, but as I stood in her presence after so much time had passed, I couldn't for the life of me regain the bitterness.

She seemed so frail. I didn't know if she'd shrunk, or if I'd gotten bigger, but as I took her in for the first time in more than ten years, I was frightened. I'd never been one for mincing words, but my throat felt as if it was closing and my breaths were shallow. Finding the courage to tell her how much she'd hurt me seemed far-fetched. Fear gripped me.

"Do you want to come in?" my mother asked, with little conviction. Her invitation felt forced, yet genuine. I'd made the trip. It felt stupid to walk away now.

"Okay," I agreed.

She opened the door wider and I stepped up, our bodies nearly touching because the entryway was so small. I always thought I'd feel the need to hug her, or swing my arm around her, but it was the exact opposite. I pulled my shoulders in, and tucked my hands into the pockets of my jeans, not wanting the contact. It was as if there were some invisible wall—something that had the power to hurt both of us if we crossed it. It was awkward, and I fought the urge to head back to my pickup as soon as she closed the door.

We stood in her living room, staring at each other, making the room feel smaller. She broke the link first, by walking to her recliner and taking a seat. She nodded toward the couch. I wanted to look around as I sat on the sofa, but fought the urge.

She folded her hands in her lap. "I don't know what to say," she said as she fidgeted. Her fingers worked a mile a minute, twiddling with the rose ring on her finger.

"Neither do I." I would have given my left nut to have had access to a time machine. Nothing about it felt normal, or even partially comfortable. "I just wanted to check on you. Make sure you were doing okay."

"I am."

"Good. Good." Like a toddler learning new words, it seemed to be the only response I could conjure. Like I'd just realized I could say it and I had nothing else in my vocabulary.

"Conner, I know this isn't pleasant." She folded her arms, like she was hugging herself for comfort. "I'm sorry I wasn't there for you."

My head tilted up, my eyes searching hers for honesty. I hadn't banked on her apologizing. Actually, I hadn't had any expectations. I think I'd been more worried about her telling me to leave and never come back. Blinking, I tried to buy more time. I was surprised, and didn't know what to say. All those years, I never counted on *her* being sorry. I just knew I was.

She faced me head on, waiting for my response. Her apology seemed honest, although she appeared to be anxious, but more in the sense that she didn't know if I'd accept.

"I know everything is messed up, and I know I'm the reason for that." I choked back my tears, forcing myself to get the words out. "I live with regret every day. I've only recently felt like I had the right to live, to succeed, to love and be loved. And for that, I'm not sorry. You have to know had I understood how my actions could affect you, I would have chosen different. Obviously, with the outcome, I would have chosen different regardless, but I just didn't have a clue what I did to you in the process.

"I've thought about it over and over, and tried to discover new ways to be forgiven, but I realized something not too long ago. I can't control anyone else. As hard as I try, I can't control how someone feels about me. And the irony isn't lost on me it took someone loving me—when I didn't feel like I deserved it—to figure it out." At the thought of Willow, I had the most peaceful sensation overtake me. I knew no matter what happened, I'd be all right.

"Conner, I'm sorry. I'm so sorry." My mother's hands gripped her face tight, holding every tear she shed in the palms of her hands. Her wails were soft, not loud in the least, but I could tell by her labored breathing and her shoulders shaking uncontrollably, she was crying.

I sat quietly, giving her a moment. As weird as it was, seeming that I was the reason for her breakdown, I felt like I was intruding on what should have been a private moment. I watched as she tried to catch her breath, then let it all out—whatever it was that had been inside her. Grief. Heartache. Guilt. Regret. I couldn't tell if it had been one, or all of them, but as sad as it was, it was also beautiful.

I was finally witnessing what I'd craved for the past decade—emotional fortitude. To know she cared. I never expected her to be okay with what happened. Disappointment would follow me forever, like a shadow, and I'd accepted that. Choices have consequences and as much as I hated it, one of those consequences would forever be a dimness orbiting my mother's heart because me.

I wanted to be the person who kept my distance from someone who'd proven they would leave me in my time of need. I wanted to be the man who turned his back to the crowd every time he won a fight, because he didn't need outside validation. I wished like hell I could have had the same wall built up in my scared heart for my mother as I'd constructed in every other facet in my life. But I couldn't. Not where my flesh and blood was concerned.

I placed a shaky hand on her shoulder. "I'm here."

She peered up at me through swollen, red eyes, and wrapped her delicate arms around my neck. I was kneeling beside her, my shins on the dull, brown carpet, and I was still taller than she was sitting in the chair. I let her arms envelope me. I let her squeeze me as tight as she could, even though it wasn't very hard, and I closed my eyes, taking it all in. My lips trembled, emotions threatening to pour out of me. I breathed deep, focused on receiving all that my mother was willing to give me. In one gesture, she gave me all her forgiveness, and asked for mine in return. I was overwhelmed.

"I do love you. I do. I'm sorry for not being there for you, son. I'm sorry I didn't know what to do with my anger. I didn't know how to support you without supporting your choices. And I was so disappointed, Conner."

I wiped her tears with my thumbs as she leaned back to compose herself. For the first time in fifteen years, I kissed my mother. I pressed my lips to her forehead and held them there until I felt breathless. "I understand. I'm sorry I put you in that position."

"Please forgive me."

"I do, Mom. It's over. I don't want to look back."

"Me either. I've wasted so much time. Time we can't get back."

She hugged me again, only this time, all the tension dissipated, like water evaporating. Clinging to her, my muscles relaxed, my chest expanded, and I took the first invigorating breath I'd had since being sentenced—a tangible breath. One where a sigh didn't follow it, nor was there any extra weight attached to it, putting pressure on my chest.

Once we'd gotten the heavy talk out of the way, I walked around her house as she pointed out the obvious improvements that needed to be made. I told her I wanted to help. She declined at first, but I insisted, knowing it was my fault it was in such bad shape in the first place. I'd already decided to fix them, making a mental list, while trying to remember what days I had to meet with people, so I could get back here to get her home looking nice.

"You mentioned love. Are you married?" She'd walked around the subject so much, I was getting dizzy, but I was still a bit gun shy about how personal we were going to get. We'd only just talked for the first time in years, and I didn't know how much I'd be comfortable disclosing.

"Not yet. I've got a girl. Willow. I just asked her to marry me last night."

"That's wonderful. What's she like? I always pictured you with a strong-willed girl. She's not too thin, I hope. These girls today, think they have to be waif-looking." She shook her head, and I smiled.

There was my mother. The one who used to tell me to drink plenty of water before every football practice, so I didn't overheat. The same woman who told me the first time she met one of my girl-friends in high school that we'd be over within the month. She'd been right.

"She's beautiful, and kind, and caring. And yeah, she's strong. Strong enough to keep me grounded, even in the circus of the AFL."

"What's that?"

"It's a fighting league. I joined a gym when I got out, and the owner —my buddy, Steele—he's a fighter. He's taught me a lot. I just signed a contract with the league."

"That sounds dangerous. You don't get hurt do you?"

I could have lied, told her what she wanted to hear, but something inside me didn't want to give her the benefit of ignorance. I was perfectly fine with her knowing the risk I took at every fight. "Sometimes."

"What about construction? Or flipping homes? You were so good at that."

I shook my head, knowing I'd never go back to that. All of that seemed like a lifetime ago. "That was then."

We reached the front yard in silence. With those three words, I'd ended our conversation. It was for the best. I'd been up all night, driving. And given the morning we'd had, I was tired and wanted to get back to Willow. I knew I'd be facing a shit-storm with the media, and even with all that time driving, and being able to think, I still couldn't wrap my brain around the shock that it was Cyndi who had been the one to expose me. Everything, from her taking on an alias to getting close to my girlfriend, not only worried me, it blew my fucking mind.

"Here's my number." I reached into my pocket and pulled out a food receipt I'd scribbled my digits down on during the last leg of my drive, just in case.

"You're leaving?" she asked, taking the paper.

"I need to get back," I said, thinking of Willow.

"I understand." She looked up at me, shielding her eyes from the sun with her hand. "Will you come back to visit?"

"Yeah. I can do that. I'll get this place fixed up for you."

"Conner, I don't want you to come back for that."

"I know. I want to do it."

"Thank you for coming. I—it made me happy. And relieved. I'm glad to see you doing so well."

"Yeah, me too. We'll be seeing each other soon. Okay?"

I needed to see my girl. I wanted my normal surroundings. Being inside my mother's home felt foreign to me, like I'd never lived there in the first place. But maybe that's how normal people felt. Maybe it wasn't. The point was, I felt safe now. Knowing my mom was all right made me feel like I would be all right. Like whatever the future brought, I could finally welcome with open arms without feeling like a fraud. With my mother's forgiveness, I felt like I deserved it.

CHAPTER 22
WILLOW

THE FRONT DOOR CREAKED, startling me from my sleep. I rolled over, facing the doorway of my bedroom, knowing Conner was about to enter. Nerves hit my belly all at once; percolating, as beads of sweat hit my skin. Dampness caused my legs to stick to the sheets.

"Hey," he said, doubt surrounding him like a golden light in the darkness.

I turned the lamp on beside my bed and sat up. "Are you okay?"

He sighed. "I am now."

"What does that mean? Where have you been?"

He took a seat at the end of my bed, caressing my bare foot that was peeking out from the blankets. "I went to see my mom."

My eyes broadened in surprise. That was the last thing I expected him to say. "Your mom?"

"Yeah." He cleared his throat. "It was the weirdest thing. I just drove and drove, until I was parked outside her house."

"I'm sorry about Dana." I hated to bring her up, but I needed him to know I'd never betray him. I still felt so guilty about it. "I've tried to think about how to fix it. I've been so worried—"

"Shh." He pulled my legs toward him, until I was sitting on his lap. I waited, watching him cautiously. "It's okay. I'm okay with whatever happens."

"You are?"

"Yeah. You know, I've let people and events take control of my life for so long, I've doubted my purpose. Doubted the reason behind my life, and why I still had one. I've been so terrified of people finding out about my past . . ." His eyes shimmered. My gut tightened and the image of him was blurred by my own tears. "I was afraid they would think I hadn't changed." He wiped my tears, leaving his to roll down his cheeks.

"But that's not who you are." I sniffed. "One mistake doesn't define you, Conner. I know yours had detrimental consequences, but you have to accept that you are still living. I know you struggle with guilt. I can see it every day. Maybe you can do something with it though."

"Like what?"

"I've been thinking about ways to help you. And maybe speaking out about driving intoxicated—being an advocate against it—will help heal you, while keeping someone else from making the same mistake. I feel like you've been dealing with it on your own for so long, you can't see any further than the inside of your own head."

His brows tightened. "I don't know if I'm ready for something like that. I don't know if I could even do it, Wil. I don't like people."

I smiled at his truthful response. "We can go slow." I rubbed his arm. "I will do the research and we can see where you're comfortable serving. We can control the outcome here."

"You are the absolute best opportunity I've ever had." He tugged on my hair. "Even though you hate me, I love you. And you've already said yes, so you're stuck with me."

Reaching into his pocket, he pulled out a small, black box. I knew what was in it, but it didn't quell my excitement. My gaze widened as he opened the box, revealing a beautiful princess cut, diamond ring, set in white gold.

"I know I should have already had this when I asked you to marry me." He held the ring so tight, the tips of his fingers were white. "But I want to give it to you now, and I don't ever want you to take it off." His head tilted, and his movement caused me to look up at him. "Not even when I piss you off, and you want to throw me out on my ass. Never, Willow." He grabbed my left hand, pulling it into his lap. "I want it to be a part of you, a representation of me, and how I don't ever want to be without you."

I gripped the pinky of his other hand in mine, and kissed his thumb. "I promise my left hand will never be without it." He placed the ring on my finger, both of us realizing he'd guessed my size wrong. "Except for getting it sized." I smirked. "I'm glad you're home. I want to hear all about your time with your mom. But *first*, I want you to get some rest. Come to bed."

He slipped out of his clothes and slid next to me. I placed my head on his chest, relieved that he was truly okay. I knew the healing process would take some time, but he'd taken the first step. And he'd taken it on his own, which I wasn't exactly fond of, but I did realize how important it was. Especially for someone like Conner.

I closed my eyes, feeling grateful for the opportunity for him to truly heal. I wished my place could have been beside him in the moment with his mother, but deep down, in the dead center of my soul, I knew my place was behind him; supporting him, not pushing. Holding him up. It wasn't my place to do things for him, or take the brunt of his past decisions and mistakes. My place tonight, was to comfort him, and to let him know that no matter what he faced, I'd be there. I'd be behind him, always being the person waiting for him when he came home.

It had taken weeks, but once the charges had been brought forward for Mikey, we'd all learned that, in a strange turn of events, he was connected to Dana. As it turned out, Dana and Mikey had been in a relationship for years. Conner and I were shocked when two detectives stopped by the gym to deliver the news.

We sat at the edge of the cage, along with Steele, as they laid out Dana's premeditated plan for revenge. Mikey advised she had written him a letter for the first time three months before Conner was released. She'd seduced him while he was behind bars, promising him a bright future when he got out.

He also admitted that while his feelings for Dana were real, and he believed hers to be as well, he noticed after a couple of months into their relationship, she'd become obsessed with Conner. Dana constantly asked questions about Conner and kept tabs on him. She knew when he was released from prison, and what city he moved to. She'd even gone so far as following him, taking weekend trips to Boston. She had his address in her phone.

According to Mikey, Conner's decision to go pro added fuel to the flames for retribution. Dana was determined, even creating a whole new career for herself, to gain access to Conner. Mikey told the police he threatened to end things with her after a while, feeling jealous of her attention on Conner, but then she told him about her son's death. Hearing the story and Conner's connection to Dana made him angry. And while he swore it was Dana's idea to harm me, Mikey had gone along with it because he believed Conner deserved to lose the one thing he loved, the same as his girlfriend had.

Hearing the extent to which Dana and Mikey were willing to go scared me. It was apparent they both had problems far beyond what prison could solve.

While Conner and I hadn't initially had to do anything other than give our statements, and get a restraining order against the pair of them, Navie would have to go to trial because of her involvement. I worried about her, and planned on being there every step of the way, just as she'd been there for me that night.

The detectives explained that Navie's testimony could be used to build a better case. But Conner flinched when they told us I might be subpoenaed as well. I didn't want to have anything else to do with it, but if it meant punishing those who'd hurt my boyfriend and friend, I was willing to do it.

Conner left for Las Vegas one month after Dana's announcement. Unfortunately, that meant Gage and Tommy doing hourly check-ins on me since I nixed my boyfriend's idea for me to travel with him two weeks before the fight. I understood where he was coming from, but I couldn't let fear get the best of me. Besides, he and I had both had enough of the past haunting us. Our future was what I wanted to focus on.

Dialing the phone number to Triple D, an outreach program specified toward reducing the risk of drunk driving, I cleared my throat as I waited on someone to answer. I was nervous, yet eager to find something important for Conner and I to focus on. I firmly believed we'd both had too much time in our own heads.

When a female answered, I introduced myself. "Hello, my name is Willow Stevens, and I'd like to speak with your coordinator."

"This is Michelle. I'm the director here."

"Oh. Hi. Um—I'm interested in helping out." I stumbled on my words, angry that I hadn't planned what I was going to say prior to my phone call. "You know, with volunteering some," I finished.

"Great. You can come down anytime between eight and five, and speak with me personally, if you'd like. I can give you a little backstory, and let you know what areas we need the most help with."

It's now or never. "Perfect. I'll have time today, if that is okay?"

"Sounds great. Look forward to meeting you, Willow."

Touring the charity's headquarters was overwhelming, and it wasn't due to its size. It was a small building, probably a little under three thousand square feet, but there were over twenty people bustling around. Michelle met me at the front desk and was more than excited when I told her I was eager to volunteer. It was then I found out they were mostly a preventative organization, one who prompted education, first and foremost.

Michelle told me a little bit about herself and why she was personally involved. Her father was an alcoholic, and not only killed himself in an accident, but her thirteen-year-old brother too. She told me, for the longest time she wanted to do something for the cause, but never knew where to start. That is, until she came across Triple D—Don't Drive Drunk. Apparently, there were plenty of Alcohol Anonymous groups out there, but with the exception of law enforcement commercials, she'd not much heard about groups who tried to abolish driving while intoxicated.

The center ran daily, and had up to thirty volunteers who spent their days printing pamphlets, doing research, talking to families who had been affected by a drunk driver, and on several occasions, met and spoke with kids at local schools. Michelle talked about how important it was to hit the pavement, and seek out those who hadn't had a horrible experience with an intoxicated driver, because those were the people who were most naïve.

My brain went into overdrive, and my heart pumped double time. I knew with every molecule in my body, Conner's place was with this organization, speaking with the kids in the area schools. With his status and cool job, they'd be more inclined to listen to him.

"Willow, if you'd be interested, I'm speaking to a local charter school after lunch. I'd love for you to join me as my guest. You can personally hear my testimony and see what our interactions are like with a younger audience."

Oh.

Well.

Okay.

"Sure. I'd love to."

I hadn't planned on jumping in head first, but admittedly, I was fascinated. Plus, my being able to learn as much as possible before introducing Conner to Triple D would only make things easier when he asked questions. And he *would* ask questions.

I wasn't sure why I was so nervous, as I wasn't the one speaking to a crowd of three hundred teenagers. However, I relaxed a bit once I arrived and saw how enthusiastic Michelle was. Taking my seat on the bottom bleacher in the gymnasium, I watched as she gathered her paperwork and walked to the podium.

I sat quietly, as she gave a rather detailed testimony on the reasons she served with the out-reach program. It broke my heart. I felt guilty for living the life I had. It wasn't her fault, or even her intention, but knowing that I'd had it so much better than others wrecked me, because I'd wasted years thinking I had it so bad. Her story made me realize everything that had happened to me was because *I* chose it.

She hadn't.

I decided in that moment, no matter if Conner joined the cause or not, I wasn't stopping. I had to be a part of it. You could have heard a pin drop in that gym when she spoke about the abuse she'd suffered from her drunken father. And when she pulled out the copies of the 911 calls she'd personally dialed from the ages of seven to sixteen, a tear rolled down my cheek. She had over thirty pages in her hands.

I recognized the pain in her voice, because I'd lived it. Throughout my time in rehab, I accepted I was an addict. Although, it'd taken a while, because I'd always considered myself a social user. Popping pills hadn't started out as pleasure for me. It had taken me months to even know why I'd been doing it.

Using wasn't a pleasant experience for me, so I never missed it. Add in the professional guidance I'd received, and I understood my reason for touching the stuff had mostly been due to the fact I wasn't grounded. My roots weren't planted; I hadn't a clue of who I was, or who I wanted to be. When you're a blank canvas, anything and every-thing sticks to you, until one day, you're so covered up by everyone else's color, you don't have any of your own. It wasn't the life I wanted to live.

And watching this woman I'd just met, bare her soul for anyone who would listen, lit a fire inside me. Seeing the affected faces in the crowd moved something deep inside my gut, forcing me to conclude that speaking on behalf of myself, and enlightening even one person, would feed my soul. I'd been so caught up in Conner's problems, I sort of forgot to address my own. I had a past too. And even though my transgressions didn't end with someone losing their life, the scars were there. I recognized hopelessness. I understood helplessness. I wasn't proud of it, but I also knew a thing or two about not taking respon-sibility.

Beside myself at the assembly's conclusion, I was in awe of the strength Michelle conveyed. It was enviable, the way she'd turned such horrible beginnings into the life she wanted. One that she was proud of. One where she was helping others, which I was learning was kind of the point.

"Michelle, I cannot thank you enough for inviting me."

We stood in the parking lot after Michelle had thoughtfully intro-duced me to most of the staff at the school. Everyone was so nice and welcoming.

"You're welcome. I'm so glad you came."

"We're out of town this week, but after Conner's fight, I'd love to introduce you to him. I'm really excited about us being involved."

"I can't wait to meet him." She grinned.

I left the school feeling more motivated than ever. Conner and I had a chance to make a difference. There was an opportunity for us to be involved with individuals who were serving a greater purpose. I spent the next two days learning everything I could about Triple D. I knew the history of the organization. Who founded it and why. I researched their board, and read numerous articles pertaining to the positive reinforcement they'd made in reducing state statistics.

I was still thinking about it when Lena and I arrived in Las Vegas for Conner's fight. I didn't mention it though because as soon as I laid eyes on him for the first time in two weeks, my brain turned to mush. I missed him so much. My libido agreed.

He caught me in his arms, warmth surrounding me as he boosted me up and around in a circle. Happiness filled my chest. "I missed you so much!"

"Me too. God, you feel good." He kissed my lips.

"Take that shit to your room," Lena joked from behind us.

"That's the plan." Conner lifted me higher, his lips skimming my neck.

"I love you." It was as if my hands had a mind of their own, touching, caressing every inch of his face.

Conner loosened his grip, so that my body slid down his, until my feet were on the ground. He grabbed my luggage and led us to the parking garage.

Once Conner had Lena set up with her room key at the hotel, he all but dragged me to our room. I felt bad for not offering to get her settled, but she waved us off, knowing Conner wasn't going to wait long to get me alone. I didn't want to stall either, but I wasn't going to be rude about it. My boyfriend, on the other hand, didn't care one bit.

Once inside the room, he brought me to him so quickly, my flip-flops fell off. He picked me up and my luggage continued to roll past us on the tiled floor in the entryway of the room.

His lips found mine, greedy and tugging, taking everything from me, before I could offer up my own kisses. I caught up to his pace just as he was placing me on the bed.

"I hated being away from you." He slipped my T-shirt over my head, leaving me in a bra.

"I know. It seems like it's been six months." I leaned up and kissed his chin, where the cutest dimple known to man existed.

"I've been dreaming of you every night. Sometimes twice."

"Aww. Has anyone ever told you how sweet you are?"

"No."

I giggled, knowing he was telling the truth. "Well, you are."

"I can't wait to make you my wife." He pulled my body down the bed by my ankles. His hands were large enough to wrap all the way around. I played with his hair as he kissed my stomach, taking his time as he made his way down to my pubic bone. Slow, passionate kisses left goosebumps in his wake. I shivered from the chill. Closing my eyes, I reveled in the feel of him.

The stretch from my lounge pants moved over my body like silk.

"I'm going to make love to you like no other time, Willow. I thought I knew before I came here how hard it would be—being away from you." He bent my knee and brought my thigh up to his lips. "I hated every second of it. If I wasn't worried about you, I was missing you. If I wasn't needing you, I was wanting to hear your voice. Absence has not made my heart grow fonder, baby. It pissed it off. You're going to have to fly out here every week next time."

"I can do that, babe. It's just trial and error at first. It's all still so new. We will get a system down that works for us. I promise. I'm here now."

Twenty mind-blowing minutes later, Conner's body collapsed onto mine, shuddering. Sweat bound us at our chests, as I scraped my nails up and down his back softly. I sighed again; complete and total peace surrounding us.

"I can't ever go that long again," he groaned.

I kissed his shoulder. "I think we just made up for it."

"Would it be crazy if I said I was thinking I could have just gotten you pregnant?"

I pushed him back, surprised that he would bring up pregnancy when we weren't even married yet. "Uh, yeah. It would be. Don't jinx us like that!"

"It wouldn't be the *worst* thing, would it?" His hopeful expression turned me to mush, considering we'd never really discussed children before, and he was clearly telling me he wanted them. With me.

"No." I pushed his hair back from his eyes. "But I want us to be married first. I don't want to have to explain to my kids why mommy doesn't have the same last name as them and daddy."

"Fair enough."

"Yeah?"

"Anything you want, anyway you want it, Willow. Forever."

I smiled and pulled him into me for one last kiss. Being someone's top priority took me to new elevations. I was his everything. Being on a pedestal that tall made me not so afraid of reaching new heights.

CHAPTER 23
CONNER

"I KNOW what you're about to do." Willow gripped my face and pulled it to hers, as I stared Preston Fuller down. "Don't. I'm ignoring him, and I want you to as well. We don't need any distractions, Conner."

"Fine." Anger surged through me. I took two full breaths, tamping down the urge to kick the shit out of Richard's son each time he ogled Willow.

"Fine?"

"That's what I said, isn't it?" I gritted my teeth.

"Don't get testy with me. I'm only looking out for you. For us."

"Me letting an asshole eye-fuck my girlfriend isn't what's good for us."

She rolled her eyes. "You're being dramatic now."

I pointed to my chest. "I'm being dramatic?"

"Yes. You are. Preston's doing the same thing to Lena. Look." She nodded toward the crowd, where Steele and Lena sat with the rest of the media and TV personalities who were waiting for the pre-interview to begin.

"Not to sound like a dick, but I don't care about Lena. I care about you."

"Stop being a baby. Now, go out there, do your job, win the fight, then take me home, okay?"

"This isn't over." I turned my back before she could smart off. I knew my girl was only looking out for me, but unfortunately for her, a twerp acting like a pervert toward my woman wasn't something I was willing to entertain. He was going to stop, or I was going to make him. I didn't give two shits that his father was my boss. I'd already signed the contract, and it was iron-clad. If Richard wanted to go that route, then I'd lawyer up. But his spineless son was going to focus his attention on someone else, and I planned on making sure of it.

The interviews had gone as planned. They began by asking mundane questions about how each of us had prepared for the fight. And while they pretended to expect an answer they'd never heard before, both my opponent and I disappointed them by sticking to the same response every athlete always gave: hard work, sleep, and eating a healthy diet. I hadn't felt the need to elaborate on the fact that I'd just gone weeks without seeing my girlfriend, and I was ready to demolish anything and anyone blocking my path for getting us back home; back to our lives together.

My challenger, Kyle Richman, had been in the pro-circuit for a little over a year. He obviously had more experience than my two fights, but I had more to lose. Taking care of Willow was my main priority, and I wasn't about to let him, or anyone else stand in my way.

Three hours later, I entered the cage, focused on annihilating Richman. I wanted it over with as soon as possible. I scanned the crowd, searching for Willow. I smirked when I saw that she was seated next to Phyllis, my biggest fan—if her homemade signs and dedication to showing up to every fight were any indication. Hell, Phyllis waited after every bout for an autograph. But she hadn't received one until my last two fights, and most of that was due to the fact that she'd punched my fiancé in the face. Given that my gracious girlfriend was able to laugh about it now, I felt like I owed the old broad for supporting me from the beginning.

Richman came out swinging. I'd been accustomed to waiting, being patient for the perfect opportunity to get my opponent on the ground, but there would be none of that with him. If I waited too long, he'd wear me out. Already, I was beginning to struggle maintaining my breaths. They were quick, causing me to take in less air.

His next punch landed dead-on to my jaw. I heard it crack, then excruciating agony coursed through the bottom of my jaw bone. I closed my eyes tight, trying to push the pain away, so I could refocus. Appropriately, Richman didn't give me time to create a thought. He saw my discomfort, and turned it on. One, two, three, jabs to my ribs. A second strike to the side of my head. His kicks were repeated over and over, like he was working out at the gym with a bag. I took all of it, trying to regain my composure, when I heard the bell sound.

Thank God.

"Do you need medical?" Steele asked.

I shook my head.

"Your jaw looks fucked up. If you keep going it could mean permanent damage."

"I can't quit," I mumbled.

Steele nodded, understanding my stance. I would never give up on a fight. If they wanted to call it, they could, but not because I told them to. I'd deal with my jaw when it was over.

I figured Richman would get a little cocky, considering he was fighting the most talked about rookie in recent years. *Rookie* being the key word. I was positive his ego would carry him farther and farther away from reality, once he thought he would win. And just like I thought, he began to stand taller and move slower, working the crowd for show. That was my opportunity to gain leverage, and I took it.

I had him on the ground and in a choke hold before he knew what was happening. I squeezed once, and he flopped around, attempting to get loose. I squeezed a second time, feeling the air being forced out of his mouth. A third pulse from my forearms was all it took, before his neck lulled to the side, letting me know he was unconscious. The referee was down on the mat, his face fully engrossed on Richman, and within a second, he had the match called.

Success.

I let go, forcing myself to my feet, relieved, even though my face was throbbing. It almost felt like a vein had been cut off, blocking it from supplying my jaw with blood. With the win, I was able to endure it. My status in the AFL remained undefeated. I had known the whole time my contract wasn't completely contingent on the wins, but I felt like I deserved the million dollars more with each victory I placed under my belt.

I made a beeline for Willow, pushing through the security I hired to protect her.

"I'm so proud of you, babe!"

"Tha—" *Fuck!* Pain shot all the way up to my brain. Sharp, short stabs of stinging started just below my ear, then like a bolt of lightning, branched all the way to my temples.

"What's wrong?" she asked.

I pointed to my jaw then made a breaking motion with my hands. Her eyes grew wide with concern. To calm her, I hugged her tight, then kissed the top of her head even though the movement hurt like hell.

Once we'd made it away from the crowd, I was able to relax. The on-call doctor looked me over, indicating that I would have to go to the hospital. I spent twenty minutes trying to reassure Willow I'd be okay, using whatever sign language and expressions I could think of. Talking was out of the question.

The doctor taped me up and released me, giving me the opportunity to walk out on my own. That beat the hell out of a stretcher any day, so I took it. I grabbed Willow's hand, tugging her down the tunnel and past the flashing lights. I didn't speak a word to any of the reporters begging for answers to stupid questions they felt the public wanted to know. Lena and Steele brought up the rear.

"Let me drive you," Willow said as we got to the truck.

I shook my head, and winced.

Once we arrived at the hospital, Willow took over like a mother hen. She filled out my paperwork, spoke with the nurses, and advised the doctor of what medications she didn't want me to have.

I smiled on the inside, as my girl tore through the room we'd been assigned, like a tornado, making sure everything was perfect for me. She taped newspapers to the windows and closed the curtains, for privacy. She sent Lena out to get my favorite snacks, even though I couldn't eat any of them. And Steele was assigned to keep the press off our trail. Willow made him swear he would tell them I was in the best shape of my life.

I didn't understand why she was going to so much trouble for the press. I didn't give two fucks if they knew Richman had broken my jaw; I won the fight. But she didn't want my name in the press for the slightest thing, and that included being in the hospital for surgery. I let her have it. She wanted to take care of me, and I had to admit, it felt good being taken care of.

When I woke up after surgery, Willow was sitting on the side of my bed, holding my hand. She'd been there the whole time, I felt it. The love she gave me unconditionally moved me. It made me feel like I could take on the world, one giant step at a time. It made the reconciliation with my mother mean more. It made my friendship with Steele more profound. The conviction I felt, knowing I'd always have her by my side, brought out a nurturing side to me I hadn't ever believed existed. She made me want to reach my potential. To pass on the good parts of me. I grinned at the thought of becoming a father. Creating a child together, giving that child equal parts of myself and the woman I loved, the woman I cherished and respected above all others, would be the epitome of love. It would be a blessing to be brought up in that kind of home.

Looking into her eyes, knowing I was about to pass out again, I tried with everything I had to tell her I loved her, but I couldn't get anything to come out. She smiled and kissed my forehead, like she'd read my mind.

EPILOGUE

WILLOW (2 MONTHS LATER)

"I CAN'T BELIEVE I had to buy off the rack. I could kick your ass for this, Payne." Lena pulled and tugged on her hundred-dollar dress, that was just a tad too tight around her chest.

"You act like it's your wedding," Steele cut in.

"These pictures will live on *forever*." Lena was being dramatic, but loveable at the same time.

"This . . ." I kissed Conner one last time before we said I do, "is all the forever I need."

"Let's get this knocked out. I got plans," Conner said loudly, not caring who heard.

I shushed him, giggling, and put my head in his chest. Not only were our friends present, but so were both of our mothers, and my mom's fiancé. Sometimes I wished we could have kept those wires for his jaw to curb his bluntness.

Standing in front of the Justice of the Peace, while our family and friends looked on, Conner and I repeated the start of our vows that would bind us forever. I pronounced each word, feeling the weight of them, knowing no matter what came in our future, we'd both be tough enough to withstand it because of our pasts.

I stepped closer to Conner, bringing my nose just under his chin. I breathed him in as I repeated the last of my vows, promising to love and cherish him forever. I knew it to be true, and so did he. He brought his lips to my forehead, sealing my words with a silent promise to do the same. I didn't need his pinky anymore. I had his heart. And his last name.

A NOTE FROM THE AUTHOR

Thank you so much for reading my book. I hope you enjoyed it, even with the darker undertones of addiction. It's unfortunate, but addiction is a reality to so many of us. Like cancer, it's poison has touched our lives in some way or another even though we never asked for it. My heart breaks for those suffering with the nagging, whispered voice inside their heads, the tug in their gut, and the constant self-deprecating thoughts.

If you struggle with any kind of addiction, please reach out to someone. Admitting a weakness doesn't make you weak. It makes you strong and courageous. It humbles you, and softens your heart. We all need help at some point, no matter what the hardship is. The difference between asking and receiving help and not, isn't measured by where you start. It's where you finish that matters.

FINISH THIS DUET WITH STEELE'S BOOK NEXT!

Learn more at CarrieThomasBooks.com.

ACKNOWLEDGMENTS

I always struggle with this part of a book because…well, there are a lot of people to thank, and I never feel like thank you is enough.

My family. My boys. Caleb, Coby, and Ayden—you are my life. All of it. My heart is always with you.

Caleb—You're just solid. Strong when I am weak. Loving when I'm frustrated, and supportive when I'm down. You understand the point of being a partner. You get it, and you've taught me so much over the last twenty-six years. I'm grateful for that. I love you so much and no matter how many times I thank you for helping me raise our kids and being such a great influence to them, it will never be enough.

Coby, I'm so proud of who you've become. Solid, loyal, and smart; you're going to do great things. I love that you have such a tender heart on the inside, but you're so tough on the outside. It makes me feel special, like I know a part of you that even your closest friends don't know about. I love you. I'm so excited to see what you accomplish in this next phase of your life. You're an adult now… and I'm middle-aged. Thank you for being a great son. You make me proud —every day.

Ayden, you are such a light in the world we live in. Always caring and grateful for everything you have. Your talent knows no bounds. There is almost nothing that would surprise me about you, and I adore that. You're funny and are always looking out for those around you. People like you are rare. Thank you for making me laugh—even when your jokes are full of teenage humor. I'm so proud of you. Thank you for being a great son. I love you.

Mom and Dad, I love you. Thank you for being the kind of parents who always supported us, and let us be who we were. You don't often think about how awful it would be to spend your whole life with someone trying to change you until you become a parent yourself. Well, I'm there… and there are times where I start to say something to one of the boys, but always think about how you didn't. Thank you for that example. I love you.

My sisters. CP and Carlos… I'm running out of words. I don't ever want to live in a world where you two don't exist. That's the short of it. I love you both. Thick and thin. Ride or die… we never give up. We stick together and we pick each other up when we are down. I have a built in support system and a couple of best friends out of the deal…so we're not changing anything.

Melinda, I love you. That is all.

ABOUT THE AUTHOR

Carrie Thomas is the author of young adult and new adult romances. When she's not writing or reading, you can find her traveling or going to concerts with friends. Museums, theater, and music are at the top of her list when traveling to a new place. Writing romance is her favorite genre to write because everyone can relate to it. She lives in the South with her husband, two sons, and a dog named Oscar De Loya Meyer Weiner. She's a firm believer that book lovers should stick together.

Learn more about Carrie Thomas at CarrieThomasBooks.com.

Sign up for her newsletter and stay connected at CarrieThomasBooks.com/Newsletter.